Amarias Adventures™

Secret of the Giants' Staircase

Amy Green

Published by Warner Press Inc, Anderson, IN 46012
Warner Press and "WP" logo is a trademark of Warner Press Inc.

ISBN: 9781593177003 (Print Version)
ISBN: 9781593174896 (E Version)

Editors: Karen Rhodes, Robin Fogle
Cover by Curtis D. Corzine
Design and layout: Curtis D. Corzine

Printed in the USA

Chapter 1

Demetri was seeking to kill four young people whose names he did not know.

Yes, he had seen three of them back in Da'armos. The tall, silent archer, the spirited girl and the cripple with the green eyes who would not betray the members of his squad. The fourth, their captain, remained both nameless and faceless in Demetri's mind.

Demetri and his companions, Ward and Lillen, referred to the Youth Guard members only as "the Four." It made Demetri uneasy, knowing so little about them. He was used to having pages of neatly recorded information about the criminals he pursued. He liked knowing exactly who they were, where they lived and what they had done that deserved death.

But the Four have done nothing to deserve death.

Demetri ignored the thought. He had gone too far to turn back now. Some choices could never be taken back.

Still, there was something strange about pursuing a nameless enemy, something almost cowardly.

Demetri was no coward. Those who resented his high position in the Patrol at such a young age called him many names behind his back, but a coward was never one of them. Back in his days as commander of a desert outpost, he had led charges into rebel camps, pursued outlaws for days with few provisions and rushed into strongholds, even if none of his men followed. It was as if he didn't care if he lived or died, others said, marveling.

They couldn't have known how right they were.

Never before had Demetri lost to an opponent of any kind. The Four, whatever their names might be, were very clever. Perhaps more than that—they had escaped death countless times. They had help of some kind. Lillen and Ward had mentioned that much at least, though they would tell him little else.

"Who are they?" he had asked Lillen the night before. "These Four who will not be defeated? Tell me their names."

"No," she insisted. She was brushing out her blonde hair with a silver brush, an action that seemed out of place in their ramshackle camp. "If you hear their names, you will begin to see their faces. Once they have faces, they will haunt your dreams. They will beg you to show mercy, and you will pity them."

"Then why do you know their names?"

Lillen set down her brush but continued to stare blankly into the darkness beyond the camp. "I see no faces," she said, her own face hard as stone. "I hear no pleading voices. And I feel no pity."

It chilled Demetri to hear those words—and from a woman, no less, one who should have a heart of compassion, a mother's heart.

Without warning, Demetri saw the face of his own mother in his mind, the way he always remembered her: long, light brown hair, laughing and turning her face toward the light as she watched the sun rise. He had always resented that his brother looked more like his mother than he did.

Now is not the time, he thought, shaking the memories away. It was dawn, but years had passed since he welcomed the sun with his mother. Now, dawn meant the breaking of camp for a new day of travel.

There was movement in the camp. Ward was fussing about something, as usual. Lillen, at once beautiful and dangerous, was rolling up her tent with a practiced hand.

Demetri did not offer to help her, though he had finished packing his own tent. Lillen was independent, and she seemed to resent any offers of help from others.

"Another wet night," Ward sighed, hefting up his pack. His slight frame bowed under the weight, but he never asked for help either—only complained about the rigors of travel until they made camp for the night.

It's a wonder we are able to maintain any kind of pace with him in our group, Demetri thought.

"I swear, the extra weight from our soaked canvas will only sink us deeper into the swamps with every passing day," he declared.

"Peace, Ward," Lillen said, standing. Though she too was slender, she bore the weight of her pack without any sign of strain or weakness. "Tomorrow we will enter the swamps to search for the Four. Today, we go to the outlying villages."

It was spoken not as a plan, but as a reminder of something they had already discussed. Demetri recalled no such conversation. "And when did we decide this?"

"I believe it was while you were on your watch last night," Ward said, giving a casual shrug. Once again, they had kept information from him, just as they did whenever they spoke of the Four, or of the prophecy or any other matter of importance for the Guard Riders.

They are on my side. We must work together, Demetri reminded himself. He breathed deeply. "And what will we be doing in these outlying villages?"

"Buying supplies, for one," Ward said, in that same self-important tone that Demetri had found infuriating after nearly a week of travel. "Describing the Four to the villagers, for another."

"They are mostly Kin," Lillen added. "Slow to get involved in the affairs of outsiders, but responsive to bribes. And they will care little about why we want to kill the Four. That is to our advantage."

"Kin?" Demetri asked. Ward gave him a superior look, which Demetri ignored. He was willing to risk looking ignorant by asking questions if the answers were worthwhile.

"An ethnic group that once lived only in this region of District Two near the swamps, but spread throughout the kingdom," Ward said, as if he were reciting from a recent census report.

Which, Demetri thought, *he probably is.* That sounded like the type of reading Ward might do to relax before going to sleep.

"They are wanderers, nomads, with a particular talent for acrobatics and other creative endeavors," Ward continued blandly. "No ties to any one place, but the strongest of ties to each other. Though they live in Amarias and pay tribute to the king, they have their own laws, pay their own community taxes, have their own leaders. It is almost as if they are citizens of another land."

"And we can buy their allegiance easily enough," Lillen said. "I thought it wise to set a reward for the Four. If they flee the swamp before we find them, or if, somehow, they escape us—"

"You are preparing for failure," Demetri said, stiffening. He hated failure. His strategy was always the same: plan for success, and plan so carefully that the only result could be success.

"You have failed before," Lillen said simply. She did not seem to be bothered by the anger in Demetri's eyes or the tightening of his fists. "We are stronger together, the three of us, but there is no reason to assume that the Four will not evade us. The Kin will stop them if we cannot."

"And you will tell *them* their names?" Demetri demanded.

"Of course," Ward snapped. "It would mean nothing to them, and might help them identify the Four."

"Then you will trust *them* with information that you will not tell me."

Lillen and Ward gave no answer.

"Well then, lead the way," Demetri said, picking up his own pack. It hardly felt heavy to him at all. "Lead me to these Kin, who will do what the king's trained Guard Riders fear they cannot."

Demetri didn't say a word the rest of the morning. It was better that way. Ward filled the air with talk of history and botany and topography of the area, as if the swampland was an artifact to be studied instead of dangerous territory to be crossed. Although he knew Ward probably thought he ignored the lecture, Demetri heard and memorized every word.

Facts were essential. They were not all that was needed for success, but pity the one who rushed into a dangerous mission without sufficient information.

Demetri had been that fool once, and it had cost him dearly.

Lillen, like Demetri, wasn't afraid of silence. She spoke only when necessary, guiding them to the first of the encampments near the swamp.

Demetri couldn't call it a city, not really, because the community was primarily made up of wagons, colorfully painted and ringed in a large circle, as if the entire group could pick up and move at any point. As they walked into the circle, though, he noticed the grass had grown long around the wheels of the wagons. It had been a long time since this particular group had relocated.

It was strange. There were people around: children playing, women doing the wash, two old men repairing a wagon. Yet no one spoke to them. No one tried to sell them wares or offered to bring them to an inn. They only stared at the strangers, clearly noting them as intruders, and went about their business. It was as if they were invisible, walking through the people instead of among them.

Suddenly, Ward stopped. "Talk to that one," he said, pointing.

A young man around Demetri's age was carrying a string of onions over his shoulder. He had deeply tanned skin, thick black hair, and a confident walk. Demetri had seen the same walk in many new recruits before the desert broke them down.

Without another word, Lillen hurried over to him. Demetri was struck with the silent, graceful way she moved, like a breeze through the trees. It seemed to startle the young man, because he jumped when she placed a hand on his shoulder.

"Why him in particular?" Demetri asked Ward, still watching Lillen.

"He strikes me as one who is susceptible to greed, and therefore, to a bribe."

"How do you know that?" All he saw was a young man carrying onions.

"As I said before, I served on the Council that divided the Youth Guard into squads. I quickly learned to understand people in little more than a glance. Most people display their virtues and faults to the world, rather like laundry blowing in the open air."

Demetri couldn't resist asking, "And what are my virtues and faults?"

"Are you sure you want to know, Captain?" Ward asked

Demetri was sure he saw a slight mocking smile appear on Ward's face."I asked, didn't I?" Demetri snapped. He wasn't used to others defying his orders.

"Why is anyone chosen for the Guard, Demetri?"

Demetri was not feeling cooperative. He had asked a question. He expected an answer, not a series of riddles. "You were the one who served on the Council, Ward. You tell me."

"Physical strength, yes, at times. Or agility, a quick mind, swiftness, fortitude, even creativity. All of those outer signs, we train those at the musters to look for, but there is another quality that almost all Youth Guard possess: a noble spirit."

"And what does that mean?"

"An inner resolve, the willingness to sacrifice and take a stand based on personal convictions—these make up a noble spirit. It's quite obvious, once you know how to look for it." Ward's face twitched into a superior smile. "And you have it, Demetri. When misdirected, it is a great weakness. A noble spirit can cause you to take unnecessary risks and make foolish, emotional decisions."

Demetri laughed bitterly. "Never again. Any nobility you sense in me must be some trace remnant from my past. Nobility is not a weakness in Captain Demetri. Only Justis."

It was hard for Demetri even to speak his real name, the one he had gone by before...*before the Youth Guard. Before the betrayal.*

"And where is Justis now?" Ward said, dark eyes staring probingly at him.

"I killed him," Demetri said tonelessly. "Long ago."

"Good," Ward said, turning his attention back to Lillen and the young man. "Yes, he will be a good one. There will be others, of course. One hundred sceptres per head is payment enough for anyone, I would think."

If he was looking for a reaction of surprise, Demetri refused to give it to him, although the price was incredible. "Wouldn't a smaller sum be enough of a temptation?"

"Believe me, Captain, we have much greater amounts of money at our disposal," Ward said casually, a small smile spreading over his face. "Riches beyond your imagination, riches that even the ancient Lidians would consider a threat."

"Lidians?" Demetri asked.

"Ancient history," Ward said. "They lived in this area. Their kingdom—or, rather, the fortress they called a kingdom—was deeper in the swamps, where they could hide from the rest of the world. Before their fortress collapsed and they fled from their home, they were the wealthiest civilization this land has ever known."

Demetri could not deny that talk of riches appealed to him. His father had been relatively wealthy, of course. *But to be able to toss around four hundred sceptres like it was nothing at all....*

Lillen had stopped talking to the young man and moved on to an old woman in a bright purple shawl. "The town gossip, no doubt," Ward said, nodding in approval. "Lillen can spot the most likely ones easily enough."

Demetri stared at the grandmotherly woman, bent and frail. "You really believe she'll give up the Four? After all, they're hardly more than children."

"I know she will," Ward said. "These people care nothing about those who are not Kin." He pointed to the scar on his jaw, a thick, jagged line of raised flesh. "It was one of the Kin who gave me this."

"A sword?" Demetri asked. A cut like that could only come from a person attempting to give a death blow.

Ward shook his head. "A dagger. It barely pierced my skin," he said, tracing the scar with one thin finger.

"That's not possible," Demetri said. He knew how to recognize a lie. He had often called out boasters on inaccuracies in their wild stories told around the Patrol watchfire. Yet this was the first time he had accused someone of minimizing his story of injury and adventure. "It would take a deep cut to leave such a scar."

"Not if the blade was tainted with a poison," Ward said. "How fortunate for me that it was not enough to be deadly." His eyes seemed to turn darker. "And how fortunate that I killed the man and took the vial of poison from his dead body."

He tugged on a cord around his neck, pulling out the Guard Rider medallion, identical to Demetri's. The symbol of the king was inscribed in it: the letter *A* inside a broken circle. But, dangling alongside it was a slim vial with a dark liquid inside.

"I keep the poison still," Ward said, lowering it beneath his shirt, "in case the need to use it ever arises."

Demetri didn't like the way he spoke those words, and he was no man to back down from conflict. "Is that a threat, Ward?"

"Yes, Captain," Ward said simply. "Those of a noble spirit are most...unpredictable. If I ever sense that you are no longer on our side, I will not hesitate to kill you. Neither would Lillen. Your choice to betray us would be your last."

With that, he walked away, leaving Demetri standing alone.

He hardly spoke a word to either of his companions as they continued their journey. They visited three groups of Kin that day, all camped near the swamp, and all distantly hostile. In every place, Lillen and Ward surveyed the people to find the "likely ones," and Lillen spoke to them of the reward. At least, Demetri assumed she spoke about the reward. Ward never let Demetri get close enough to hear what she said.

The Four would die nameless, then. There was no question that they must die. Demetri had pledged himself to the Guard Riders, sworn to destroy the Youth Guard. Aleric, the captain of the Riders, would punish him for another failure. And Ward had made it clear that turning back was no option.

As they left the last Kin encampment, Demetri felt the power of the Rider medallion he wore. He reached up to touch it. It gave him strength, somehow, and reassured him that he would enter the swamps and come out alive.

But the Four, the nameless Four, would not.

CHAPTER 2

When Jesse turned his boots upside down, there were twin holes in the heels. "Silas," he groaned loudly. "Is the entire surface of your district made of jagged rock?"

Silas, already getting out the fishing line, didn't seem bothered by Jesse's comment. "Your district has grassland and mud. Mine has rock and—"

"More rock," Rae added, when Silas couldn't think of anything to finish the statement. She tapped her leather boots. "But blame the makers of your shoes, Jesse, not the land we've crossed. Mine are just fine."

Jesse rolled his eyes. "A fine lot of support I get around here. I'll have you know these boots were made for farm work, *not* for climbing over every rocky trail in the kingdom of Amarias."

"Never fear, Jesse," Parvel said, clapping him on the back, which nearly knocked him off the boulder he rested on. "District Two also has a very fine swamp—one that I hope we will be approaching very soon."

He directed this last comment at Silas, who nodded. "Two

days journey, perhaps. Maybe less."

Jesse wasn't sure if this was good news or not. According to the Forbidden Book, the swamps were the last place one of the missing Youth Guard squads had been seen alive. When they reached the edge, they would have to enter and find them, facing unknown dangers along the way. Even Silas, who had grown up in District Two, knew very little about the swamps. *Or, at least, he's telling us very little.*

The thought had crossed Jesse's mind more than a few times that Silas might know more than he said, afraid of frightening them. *But after all we've seen in the last month, what could be worse? Besides, we don't have a choice. If we don't go into the swamp, the other squad will die.*

"I can't wait until we get something to eat besides fish," Rae said, scowling at the stream next to them. Their supplies, borrowed from Prince Corin, had only lasted a few days. For the past week of traveling, they had followed the river, eating fish from the stream for dinner.

"I can fix it a little differently this time," Parvel offered hopefully.

"No," they all said at once. The night before, Parvel had garnished the fish with a red sauce. The fish had been halfway to Jesse's mouth when Silas asked him what he had used. It turned out to be bloodberries. Jesse had immediately dropped the fish and threw it into the fire. Even the smoke smelled toxic.

"He could have just poisoned us all and saved the king the trouble of killing us," Silas had muttered while washing off his plate.

Hearing him say that reminded Jesse exactly how serious their situation was. Sometimes, fishing with Silas in the dusk, he forgot that a Patrol division could march out of the woods and kill them, leaving them in unmarked graves along the road.

They'd have to go a distance to find a road, though. That was Parvel's idea. "Chancellor Doran must know we're alive by now," he had said the day they set out from Davior. "He'll send someone after us. We should go the long way to the swamp, avoiding main roads and all towns."

That was why they were still two full days away from the swamp after a week of travel. Every morning, Jesse would wake up achingly stiff, only to face another long trek over rugged terrain.

But it's worth it if it keeps us alive. And, anyway, I'm getting used to the hard travel, Jesse thought. His skin was darker from hours in the sun, and if he wasn't mistaken, he was developing a bit of muscle. Not on his crippled left leg, of course, but the other was growing twice as strong.

"Come on, Jesse," Silas said, jerking his head toward the river. "Let's catch dinner."

Jesse took out the leather cord and makeshift hook that served as his fishing pole. All the poles he had ever owned were handmade, but this one took the prize for the most crude—pieced together from odds and ends they had brought with them from Roddy's tavern and Prince Corin's store of supplies.

Silas was already by the water, perched on a mossy boulder. "What's the score?" he asked Rae.

She sat on the bank a distance from the water, as usual. Jesse knew it was because she was afraid of water, but none of them ever mentioned it. *The first person who does*, Jesse thought, *will probably get punched.*

"Jesse eight, Silas three," Rae recited.

Don't be smug, Jesse commanded himself. Still, he couldn't help but grin a bit. It was nice, for once, to be better than Silas at something—anything. Silas, Rae and Parvel were the real Youth Guard members, chosen for their strength, intelligence and bravery. He was just a cripple who had come along on their adventures.

But he was a cripple who knew how to fish.

He ambled over to the river, tying the cord to the end of his staff—a bendbow knot, his father had called it.

Jesse felt a stab of pain at the memory. Sometimes, when they were running for their lives or involved in a mission, he almost forgot about his parents. But not quite. He didn't know where they were or if they were even alive, just that they disappeared a year ago. He hadn't heard from them since.

The Forbidden Book gave them information about the lost, but only lost Youth Guard members. Jesse wished the book were magic and could tell him where to find any person he named. It had been a long time since he and his father had gone fishing together.

With a sigh, Jesse plopped down on the bank, sticking his feet in the river and swirling them around. The cold water felt good on his sore feet.

"You'll scare off the fish," Silas warned him. When he fished, he always sat in complete silence, hardly moving at all. Sometimes, Jesse thought he was dead, until he saw him blink.

"Apparently, I haven't been scaring them off," Jesse said, smirking. "Just scaring them right onto my hook."

Silas shook his head, and Rae scoffed out loud.

"Anyway, I'm not fishing yet," Jesse continued. "I'm just watching the currents."

"Watching the currents," Silas repeated skeptically.

Jesse nodded. "Old trick from District One," he said. "You've got to know how to time the currents. That's how I catch all my fish." He shrugged and tapped his staff with its intricately carved designs, a gift from his friend Kayne. "And my staff brings me good luck."

"I thought you Christians didn't believe in luck," Silas said. Even though it was a simple comment, Jesse could hear the bitterness in his voice.

He decided it wasn't the time to start yet another argument about God. Those always went the same way. He and Parvel against Silas and Rae, all repeating the same arguments and neither side changing their minds. "I was joking," Jesse said. "Fishing is pure skill."

Rae gave a little half-snort at that, and Parvel chuckled warmly. He was setting up a brush pile to start their small cooking fire.

"I think I'll go upstream a bit," Jesse said, leaning on his staff.

Silas didn't complain. He never did. Jesse had counted on that. *He probably enjoys the peace and quiet.*

Jesse found a shallow part of the river, where the muddy

bottom was higher and current slower. He took one glance back to make sure no one had followed him. Then he pulled his net from underneath his shirt.

His father had taught him how to catch fish in a homemade net. It was quicker and easier than waiting for fish to bite on a line, and the materials could be found on nearly every riverbank in Amarias. All Jesse needed was waterflax, a thin reed that grew in patches all along the riverbank.

The long days of walking had given him plenty of time. With his crippled leg, he was always the last one in the group. If the other members of his squad thought it was strange that he braided reeds as he walked, they never said anything.

It had taken him three days to make the net. It was a bit like a basket, only more flexible, with a looser weave. True, it wasn't strong enough to hold much weight. *But small fish can be cleaned, baked, and eaten just as well as large ones.*

He knelt down on the very edge of the bank, making sure his shadow was behind him. Any movement could startle the fish. Then it was a waiting game. Jesse carefully studied the water, waiting to see a fish poke out of the weeds. *Dinner should be here any. . . .*

All of a sudden, he was tumbling face-first into the water. He came up, sputtering and wiping the wet hair out of his eyes, grabbing at the bank to pull himself out.

There, shaking her head at him, was Rae. "Pure skill, hmm?" she said, hands on her hips.

Jesse gave her a weak smile. "Yes?"

For one wild, crazy second, he thought about pulling her in with him. Then he checked himself. *Do I want to die?*

Since the answer was no, he just floated there, doing his best to look repentant when what he really wanted to do was burst into laughter.

She just shook her head and marched back toward their camp. Jesse quickly stood and sloshed over to her. "It wasn't cheating," he said. "I made the net myself. I caught the fish myself."

But she didn't even slow down. "Then you won't mind if the others hear about your stroke of brilliance."

Actually, Jesse wouldn't mind. He was rather proud of it and was planning to tell Silas eventually. "You made me lose my fish, by the way."

"I don't care," Rae said. "Now, move away. You're getting that dirty lake water on me."

"It's a river, Rae," Jesse said, rolling his eyes, "not a lake."

"It's not well water," Rae fired back, walking faster. "That's all I care about."

Unlike in District One and Two, where most children learned to swim shortly after they learned to walk, residents of District Three avoided water whenever possible. As to why, all they could get out of Rae was mention of some old superstition. She always ended those conversations as soon as possible.

They had reached the camp. "She's delusional," Jesse cried in protest, running ahead of Rae. "It's the journey—it's just too much for her. Don't listen to anything she says."

Parvel and Silas just stared at them. "Anyone feel like explaining?" Parvel asked.

Rae was only too happy to volunteer, going into great

detail about Jesse's net.

"So that's how you caught so many," Silas said, shaking his head. "Is that really fair, Jesse?"

"Yes," Jesse said. "We were keeping track of how many fish we caught. No one said *how* we had to catch them."

"True enough," Parvel said, "however, for acts of deception and general braggery—"

"I don't think that's a word," Jesse interrupted.

"As squad captain, I officially sentence you to the chore of gathering the rest of the firewood for tonight's meal," Parvel pronounced solemnly.

Jesse made a face. In the rocky terrain that was a hard task. The trees that grew in the shallow mountain soil were mostly varieties of pine. It was backbreaking work to collect dead branches scattered on the ground.

"Fine," Jesse said, taking the hook and line off of his staff, "but you realize that leaves Silas in charge of catching our dinner. And we know he doesn't have the best record...."

"I'll do just fine," Silas said coolly. He had never taken his line out of the creek. "And I'll do it without your fancy net."

By the time the sun was low in the sky, they had a nice river flateye to share. As usual, Jesse and Parvel prayed over their meal, but Silas and Rae did not.

"Eat quickly," Silas said, glancing at the sun. "It's almost dark, and we need to put out the fire."

Jesse knew why. They never lit a fire after sundown. Anyone passing by could see it from a distance, although the rocky terrain worked in their favor. Silas suggested never starting a fire at all, but when the others objected that raw fish were not very appetizing, he settled for making the fire as small as possible.

As soon as they finished eating, Silas poured water on the fire, making the coals hiss and sputter. He started to throw dirt on them to smother them.

"Can't we keep the fire going?" Jesse protested. "I'm still wet!"

"I'm sorry," Silas said, not sounding sorry at all, "but I value our safety over your comfort."

"And you deserved that trip into the river anyway," Rae added bluntly. Jesse just shook his head, sprinkling her with water and earning a look of disgust.

"Well, the good news is, I patched your shoes," Parvel interrupted, holding them up.

Jesse took them and turned them over. There, stuffed into the holes, were two rocks.

Jesse threw one of the shoes at Parvel's head, but for being so burly, Parvel could move quickly. He ducked, and the shoe plunked into the river.

"Next time, I'm throwing the rock," Jesse threatened, limping over to the river as quickly as he could to fish the shoe out.

"With your aim, I doubt I should worry."

"Thanks a lot," Jesse grumbled, but Parvel's deep, rumbling laughter drowned him out.

He marched back and dropped the shoe, rock and all, next to the dying fire. "Goodnight," he proclaimed, making a show of shivering as he lay on the ground, covered only by his blanket. They had lost their tents long ago, back in the Rebellion headquarters. "Wake me up for my shift on watch."

"Oh, I will," Rae said. He always followed her during the night watch. "Maybe even a little early tonight." She gave a loud yawn that was clearly fake. "I'm very tired, and I know I can count on you to be a gentleman, Jesse."

Jesse just moaned and wrapped his blanket tighter against his damp clothes. "Nice to know I'm falling asleep among friends."

And, though he wouldn't have believed it a month before, it really was true.

CHAPTER 3

The next night, Jesse remained exiled from fishing duties; however, that didn't stop Silas and Parvel from borrowing Jesse's net. They had gone a distance down the river to use it. Silas said it was because the river was too fast where they had made camp. Jesse suspected Silas didn't want him to watch and taunt him if he missed his first few tries.

"He's so used to being perfect at everything he can't stand making a mistake like every other human," he muttered to himself.

He had to admit, though, that the four of them made a good team. *We might even be the best squad in Youth Guard history,* he thought. *How else could we have stayed alive for so long?*

"Come on," Rae said, jerking him away from his thoughts. "Time to prepare the fire. We want to be ready when Silas and Parvel come back."

"Even with my net, they might not be able to catch anything," Jesse said.

"Don't be cocky," Rae shot back. "You're not the only one who can use that contraption."

"That's not what I meant," Jesse said, pointing to the angry storm clouds gathering above them. "Looks like rain. Even if Silas and Parvel come back with fish, we may not be able to make a fire to cook them."

"I've eaten raw fish before," Rae said, shrugging. "In training. It can be done."

Jesse wondered if she was saying that to impress him, or if she really would eat raw fish. Just the thought of it made him sick.

"It's your turn to gather firewood," Jesse reminded Rae, who had sat down on the grass. She was whittling the bark off a stick with her dagger.

"Here's a deal for you. You get the firewood. I'll patch your boots."

"Can you do that?" he asked doubtfully.

Her eyes flashed, and the dagger moved even quicker over the wood, slicing longer strips of bark. Jesse was afraid she was going to cut one of her fingers off. "Why? Do you think all I can do is fight?"

Jesse shook his head quickly. "No. It's just that mending things seems so...." He searched for a word that wouldn't make Rae angry and couldn't find one.

"My mother taught me a few things, thank you," Rae said, rolling her eyes.

Jesse took off his boots and handed them to her without any more comments.

Today, unlike the previous night, it was an easy task for Jesse to find wood. As the day wore on, they had finally left the rugged terrain behind. Now, in place of jagged rock, groves of trees dotted the riverside. Silas had promised them that they would reach the swamp soon.

When Jesse came back with a bundle of wood a quarter of an hour later, Rae already had rags fitted into the hole of one shoe and was cutting cloth to fit the second.

Jesse watched her for a while, then set down the wood and started arranging stones to form a firepit. *Stones are one thing we have plenty of in this district.* "Thank you," he said to Rae when she handed him the boots.

"My back was sore from gathering firewood every night," Rae said with a shrug.

Jesse knew that was a lie. Rae never got sore or tired or hurt. At least, that's how it seemed to Jesse. He guessed she just wanted an excuse to help him.

He sat and put the boots on. "There's a thin layer of bark to keep water out," Rae told him.

"Good idea," Jesse said.

Rae just shrugged again, but Jesse could tell she was proud of her handiwork.

"Greetings," a low voice said. Rae gave a short gasp of surprise.

Jesse whirled around. Walking casually out of a grove of trees, was a young man with black hair and tanned skin. He was dressed in a tunic with a strange, circular design dyed in it. Jesse had the feeling he had seen it somewhere before.

"Good day," Jesse said, forcing himself to sound cheerful.

The stranger looked them over carefully, raising his eyebrows. Jesse didn't like the suspicious cast in his eyes. *He seems...oily, somehow. Yes, that's a good word. Like the grease slicking back his hair.*

"What are you doing alone in these parts, so far away from the main road?"

"My brother and I were fishing," Rae blurted.

Jesse groaned inside. Rae was not a very good liar. They didn't look like they could be remotely related—Rae with her dark hair and pale skin, and Jesse with brown hair and green eyes.

"You're brother and sister?" the stranger said, arching his eyebrows again.

"Yes," Rae said firmly.

"She's my half-sister, actually," Jesse offered lamely.

"And where are you headed?" the stranger asked. "I might be able to give you directions. You seem to have wandered off the main road."

For a moment, Jesse froze. He didn't know the name of any nearby towns. Then Rae spoke up. "To the swamps," she said.

The stranger frowned. "Are you sure that's wise? They call them the Swamps of the Vanished for good reason. Those who go in...." He shrugged, but Jesse knew the end of this sentence. *Never return.*

Just then, Silas and Parvel ran into the clearing. "Rae, we—" Parvel began. He froze when he saw the stranger.

"Are they your brothers too?" the stranger asked. His eyebrows were up permanently now, and something about his bland stare made Jesse squirm uncomfortably.

"It's none of your concern," Rae said hotly. She moved her hand toward the dagger at her side. Jesse prayed she wouldn't have to use it.

Parvel and Silas were unarmed, their weapons in their packs. *Could I sneak over and grab a sword? Even if I could, would I use it?* The thought of killing a man, even one who seemed to be a threat, made Jesse sick.

The stranger began to pace, smiling to himself. "I know who you are. Four young people, alone in the wilderness. Not wanting to be seen. Lying about your identity."

With every word he spoke, Jesse's heart beat faster. *What do I do? Should we run? Should we fight?* The man didn't seem to be armed, but Jesse knew from experience there were a hundred ways to conceal a weapon.

"Again, it's none of your concern," Rae repeated. "Leave us be."

"None of my concern?" The stranger stopped short and gave Rae a look of mock disapproval. "Why, I'm a citizen of Amarias. Shouldn't I be concerned when I discover four young people who are wanted for treason?"

With a cry, Rae reached for her dagger…but there was nothing there.

The stranger held it out, twirled it in the air and caught it again. "Looking for this?"

"Yes," Rae said. At the same time, she struck the stranger in the face with her fist and grabbed for the dagger.

"Rae," Jesse yelled, lunging forward.

But the stranger had already broken her grip and turned the dagger on her instead, holding it against her throat. Parvel and Silas rushed to their weapons, but it was too late.

"Hold!" the stranger called. "Put down your weapons, fools!"

"And what makes us foolish? That we would defend our sister?" Parvel demanded. He and Silas were just paces away from their weapons, but made no move toward them.

"No more lies," the stranger snapped. "I know who you are. You called the little one Rae. The two of you are Silas and Parvel, and the crippled one is Jesse."

"How do you know our names?" Jesse asked. Even if the stranger suspected they were Youth Guard, he could not know who they were. And if he were one of the king's men, sent to destroy them, Rae would already be dead.

"Come with me," the stranger said. "I can do nothing without consulting my father and the Kin."

"Then you can't order us to follow you, can you?" Jesse pointed out.

"If you come peacefully, I won't harm you," the stranger continued, ignoring him, "despite the king's promise of reward for your death or capture."

"Reward?" Jesse asked, curious in spite of himself.

"Yes. A very large sum, in fact. One hundred sceptres…for each of you." Even Rae gasped at that. The slight movement brought her uncomfortably close to the edge of the dagger.

The stranger gave a slight smile. "Tempting, I know. A man like me could work his entire life and never see that much money. Likely that's what the Patrol captain's companions thought when they told the Kin of you. They said to watch for anyone meeting your description and turn you in."

A Patrol captain? Jesse glanced at the others. He knew there were dozens of Patrol captains in Amarias. There was no reason to assume the stranger was speaking of Captain Demetri, who had pursued them since the Abaktan Desert.

No reason except the sick feeling Jesse was getting in his stomach.

The stranger paused and held out his free hand, catching a few raindrops that were starting to fall. "Well, will you do it?" Parvel asked.

"The Kin will decide," was all the stranger would say.

By now, Jesse had decided the Kin was some kind of group or clan, maybe a local government. He had never heard of such a thing, but he was not from this district. It had not taken many days of travel to realize how different the four districts of Amarias were from each other.

"I thought you should know about the rewards, in case you tried to run or attack me." The stranger looked evenly at them. "There are others looking for you—others who are far more dangerous and bloodthirsty than I am. And they are willing to pay a very high price to make sure you are dead."

The stranger put his hand on Rae's shoulder and began to march her forward, toward the east. Then he stopped. "And don't try to take those weapons, or anything else in your packs."

Jesse decided that didn't include his staff. Somehow, the stranger knew he was crippled before he ever took a step. He would guess Jesse needed the staff to walk.

Suddenly the stranger whirled around. "I said, take nothing from the packs!"

Silas was kneeling on the ground. He was clutching the Forbidden Book.

"It's a religious text," Silas said calmly, wrapping it in his cloak to protect it from the rain. "A book of prayer."

Jesse almost laughed. *As if Silas of all people would carry a book of prayer.*

The answer seemed to satisfy the stranger, although he waited for Silas to walk ahead of them. "Keep the book close," he said, prodding them forward. "When you go before the Kin, you'll need all the prayer you can get."

CHAPTER 4

Even with the darkness of the storm, the wagons of the Kin were the most colorful Jesse had ever seen: huge wooden boxes on wheels painted with swirls of color.

That's when Jesse realized where he had seen the stranger's style of clothes before. They were the same as the costumes of a troupe of traveling performers that had once passed through Mir.

"Don't try to shout for help," the stranger warned them as they approached the wagons. He was still in the lead, holding Rae captive. "Believe me, if the others know you're here, it'll only be worse for you." With a reward of four hundred sceptres for them, Jesse was sure he was right.

They wove through the maze of colorful wagons, until the stranger stopped at a yellow one with red trim. Jesse realized he hadn't seen any tents or houses in the clearing. *These people must live in the wagons,* he realized. *No wonder the wagons are so large.*

They climbed the three steps that led to the wagon, and the stranger pounded on the door with his free hand.

"Is that you, Tomas?" a voice rumbled from behind the door. "You're back early."

The door opened, and a boy no higher than Jesse's waist stood there. Not, Jesse guessed, the one who owned the rumbling voice they had heard. His eyes went wide. "Who are these people?"

"Just let me past," Tomas said, pushing by him. "And the rest of you come in too. No sudden moves."

"They're not gonna fit," the boy warned him.

He was almost right. They all fit, but barely. Silas had to stoop slightly, so he wouldn't graze the ceiling.

Inside the wagon, the furnishings were sparse—just a few blanket rolls and a small table with two thick candles. A large dark-haired man was sitting on a bench that looked like it would crack under his weight.

When he saw his guests, a flicker of surprise registered on his face, but it was gone in the next second. "Now, son, you know that stealing brides is something the Kin gave up many generations ago," the man said. His voice was stern, but there was a warm twinkle in his eyes.

Jesse had to laugh at the horrified look on Rae's face. "I am *not*—" she began.

"Don't worry. He knows," Tomas said. He didn't look amused at his father's joke either. He released Rae and pressed himself against the door—to block any escape, Jesse assumed.

"Which one gave you that?" the boy said, pointing to Tomas' black eye.

"Nothing you need to know," Tomas snapped.

"I did," Rae said, squaring her shoulders proudly, "and there will be more coming unless you release us!"

"What's all the noise about?" A woman's voice came from beyond a curtain that separated the wagon into two rooms. "Did one of you bring in another snake?"

"Yes," Tomas said, glancing at Rae. She sniffed haughtily at him.

There were footsteps as the mother of the house ducked through the curtain. "Zacchai, I believe we already discussed—" She stopped short when she saw the Youth Guard members. "Oh my."

Jesse could tell that Tomas had gotten his looks from her. Instead of looking greasy, though, her hair was a mass of sleek, loose waves, falling most of the way down her back. She held a baby against her hip, who took one look at all the people and started to cry.

"Shh," the woman said, cradling the baby while giving the visitors a quick glance. She turned to her husband, alarm in her eyes. "It's them, isn't it?"

"Margo, I don't know what you're talking about," the husband said, yawning loudly.

"Of course not, Ravvi," Margo said, shaking her head. "You didn't join the Kin assembly yesterday when the messengers from the king came. And when I tried to tell you—"

"There was wood to split!" he protested. "Besides, I care as much for the king's men as I do for the manure heap." He spit on the floorboards to prove his point.

The baby was still crying. Rae looked about ready to jump forward and strangle it.

Margo looked straight at her son, pleadingly. "Why did you bring them here, Tomas? Why couldn't you have left them alone?"

"I did what I thought was best," Tomas said, folding his arms over his chest. "We can bring them to the meeting of the elders tonight."

"You *know* what they would do to them," Margo said, jostling the baby, who cried louder. Rae growled under her breath.

Jesse stepped over Zacchai, the boy sitting on the floor, and reached for the baby. "May I?" he asked. He was an only child, but the children in the village always seemed drawn to him.

Margo gave him a hard, searching look. *A mother's look*, Jesse thought. Then something in her face softened, and she passed the baby to him.

"The elders will turn them in to the Patrol captain," Margo finished, turning back to Tomas. "They'll put the money in the Kin treasury."

"Where it will do much good," Tomas countered.

"Not blood money," Margo said. "Blood money never brings good. Only evil."

Jesse knew "blood money" was the term used to describe money gotten from betrayal, but the phrase still sounded eerie. He remembered another story about blood money—where Judas, a follower of Jesus, turned Him over to the men who killed Him.

But they won't do that to us...will they?

Jesse rocked the baby back and forth. She—Jesse guessed the baby was a she because of the wooden flower on a bracelet around her wrist—seemed confused at first by the new face looking down at her. But she stopped crying at least.

"It's a large amount of money, Mama," Tomas said. "More than we could dream of, no matter how many performances we give. We could have the life we've always wanted."

"Then I do not want that life anymore," Margo said firmly. "Not at that cost."

"If I may—" Parvel began.

"No, you may not," Tomas said.

"Son," Ravvi said in a warning tone. "No need to be rude."

"He's threatening to sell them to their death, and you're concerned about his tone of voice?" Margo scoffed at her husband.

Jesse made a face at the baby. She giggled. "Shh," Jesse whispered. "This isn't funny." He couldn't help but smile, though.

"This is none of our concern," Ravvi said. "What the outsiders do, the laws they have or break…none of that has any place here. We of the Kin should only concern ourselves with Kin matters."

"That doesn't seem to be an option," Parvel said. "We are in your world now. You have to concern yourselves with us."

He said it like a challenge, and Jesse realized he was right. Any chance they had of survival was with this family.

"There's no going back now," Tomas said. "So, Papa, Mama, what do we do with them?"

No answer. Parvel seemed to be staring Ravvi down, but Ravvi wouldn't look at him.

"What's her name?" Jesse asked in the pause.

Jesse saw Rae roll her eyes.

"Sofia," Margo said.

"Right." Jesse turned back to little Sofia. "Your life is a lot easier than ours, isn't it?" he whispered as the argument went on. She gurgled and spit up on him. "I'll consider that a yes."

"And I agree with Tomas," Ravvi said. "This is not something we can decide alone. We must consult the rest of the Kin."

"Isn't there another way?" Margo asked. "Can't we just let them go? Pretend they were never here?"

Tomas sighed. "Mama, just because Sofia likes one of them...." He shook his head. Sofia giggled, recognizing her name.

"They're clearly criminals," Tomas continued.

"No, we're not," Rae blurted. She shot Parvel a quick glance, then continued. "We're Youth Guard members."

If they had been surrounded by the king's men, that would have been a death sentence. As it was, everyone in the room seemed to freeze, except Zacchai and Sofia. Suddenly, Tomas looked even angrier, Ravvi looked hard and distant, and Margo looked about to burst into tears.

Jesse wondered what it was about the Youth Guard that produced such a strong reaction.

"See?" Rae said, pulling up her sleeve to reveal the symbol of Amarias tattooed into her skin, the mark of the Youth Guard. "As protectors of this kingdom, we ask for your help."

"We don't owe them anything," Tomas said, still speaking to his mother. "We should turn them in as soon as possible."

"No," Margo said, and when she straightened her shoulders and stood upright, Jesse was sure she would break through the roof of the wagon. "We will do nothing of the kind." She took a deep breath. "I, too, have a son."

"Yes, we know," Rae said dryly. "He's very charming, especially holding a dagger."

"I do not speak of Tomas, or Zacchai, though they are both dear to me." Margo's face became strong again. "I am speaking of Barnaby."

Barnaby. Jesse knew that name. He was one of the four Youth Guard members they were searching for in the squad assigned to the swamps.

Ravvi stood from his bench. "He left us of his own accord, Margo, against our specific orders."

"Yes, and it was wrong of him," Margo said, "but he's just a boy still."

"Stop making excuses for him, Mama," Tomas snapped.

"I am not making excuses," Margo replied hotly. Jesse was glad he was the one holding Sofia, because her mother was gesturing wildly with every word she spoke. "Right or wrong, he is our son, and I will not give up on him."

"He gave up on us," Tomas shouted back. "Did you ever think about that, Mama? Maybe he *did* know exactly what would happen when he left. Maybe he wanted to be cut off from the Kin—from us."

The wounded expression on Margo's face made Jesse uncomfortable. He felt like they had stumbled into a family conflict and that they should excuse themselves and leave them in privacy. But Tomas still blocked the door, and Jesse was fairly sure he wouldn't be moving.

"He's probably dead anyway," Tomas said. His facial expression told Jesse the second, unspoken half of his statement: *It's no more than he deserves.*

"No," Margo said quietly, but with force. "I will not believe that. As we of the Kin say, 'Not all that is missing is gone.' Barnaby may yet come back from his foolish mission."

"Your son is in the Youth Guard?" Jesse asked, shifting Sofia in his arms.

Margo nodded. "He's been gone for more than four months."

Jesse knew that this included the three months of training in the capital city. He glanced at Parvel for guidance. "Should we tell them?"

"I don't think we have a choice now that you've spoken," Silas said dryly.

He was right. Everyone in the wagon was staring at him. "Well," Jesse asked, "where should I start?"

"At the beginning," Zacchai suggested. He looked excited, clearly sensing a story coming.

So Jesse began, "One month ago, I was cleaning tables in Mir…."

"No—" Tomas interrupted, "not at the beginning Something…sooner. And quicker."

Jesse shrugged. "Fine." One of the first rules of storytelling was always keep the audience happy. *Especially when one audience member is holding a dagger.* "We are in the Youth

Guard as you know. What you may not know is that, instead of helping us accomplish our mission, the king and his men tried to kill us."

Jesse waited for a response of surprise and alarm, the same response he had when he heard the news. Nothing happened.

"They don't care, Jesse," Rae said. "It's none of their concern, remember?"

"Oh," Jesse said. Then he remembered why he had told the story in the first place. "But it isn't just us the king is trying to kill. He's trying to wipe out every single Youth Guard member…including Barnaby."

Now Margo gasped. Even Ravvi looked alarmed.

"Mama," Zacchai whimpered, and Jesse felt a twinge of guilt about being so blunt in front of the boy. "Is Barnaby going to die?"

"Not if we can help it," Parvel said. "We have his squad's last known location. That's why we're here, and why the Patrol captain was so desperate to get rid of us. He knows we could save others."

"Why?" Tomas challenged. "If you could save yourselves and run, why find the others?"

Jesse thought for a second. "Because the Youth Guard members, all of them, are part of our Kin," he finally said.

That, he could tell, connected with them, but Tomas still stood in the doorway, arms crossed. "What if they're lying?" he asked.

Silas took out the Forbidden Book. Carefully, he paged through it until he found what he was looking for. He held up the book.

It was a sketch of Barnaby. Jesse could tell that immediately. He looked like a small version of Ravvi, a mischievous grin lighting up his face. Two feathers stuck out from behind his ear.

Margo gave a slight moan, and Jesse was afraid she was going to cry. He was never sure what to do when females cried, unless they were Sofia's age. She was currently chewing on a tassel attached to her blanket, unaware of the conflict around her.

"You must let us go," Parvel said. "We cannot promise that we will find your son, but we will die trying, if need be." Jesse knew that he meant every word.

"*We* should be going to find Barnaby," Ravvi muttered, clenching his fists at his side. "I should go."

"You know you can't, Papa," Tomas said. "The Kin could disown you too. If you leave, you leave Mama, Zacchai, Sofia and me."

"You?" Ravvi demanded, his voice rising. "You would not come with your father to save your own brother?"

Tomas didn't answer.

"We must decide," Margo said, "quickly, before the Kin meeting is called and the elders gather."

For a few seconds, no one said anything, not even baby Sofia.

Then Ravvi sighed deeply. "Go," he said. "Tomas, you will make sure they get safely away from the camp." Tomas didn't look happy with the command, but he nodded. Margo immediately ducked into another room.

"Then let's go at once," Parvel said. Jesse knew he wanted to leave before Ravvi changed his mind.

"Good-bye, Sofia," Jesse whispered. "You were my favorite."

She smiled toothlessly at him like she could understand. Jesse decided he was probably her favorite too. He handed her back to Margo, who had reentered the main room.

In exchange, she gave him a wrapped package and a small object on a leather cord. When he looked closer, Jesse could see it was a piece of wood carved in the shape of a bird. "The food is for you," Margo said, pointing to the package. "The other is for Barnaby. It's his token, the fledge bird. Each member of the Kin is given a token at birth."

Jesse put the cord around his neck. "I'll give it to him," he promised.

"And tell him to bring Zora back," Zacchai added.

"Zora?" Rae asked, frowning. "There was no one in the Youth Guard with that name."

"That's because she's a bird," Zacchai said, like Rae was a complete fool. "A fledge. Like the one on the token necklace. Only real."

"How was I supposed to know that?" Rae demanded.

"Rae," Silas said, putting his hand on her shoulder. "He's six years old. Let him win this argument."

"Come," Tomas said, jerking his head toward the door.

"Give me back my dagger first," Rae demanded.

"Not a chance."

"Son," Ravvi said, in a warning tone, "do as she says."

Immediately, Tomas gave Rae the dagger. She sheathed it

with a glare at him. Jesse guessed that disobeying a command from a parent was a serious offense in the Kin. Otherwise, he was sure Tomas would have died before giving back Rae's dagger.

They ducked out the door into the rain, falling steadily now. Jesse's staff sank down in the mud with every step. Tomas scanned in all directions before leading them out of the camp.

The others followed behind them. Jesse knew it was not because they couldn't keep up, but because at training camp they were taught never to let an enemy walk behind you. Jesse didn't care. He was sure Tomas wasn't a threat anymore, in spite of his bluster.

"I always knew Barnaby would do something like that eventually," Tomas muttered.

Jesse guessed it would be better not to ask questions or say anything at all. He just kept pace with Tomas and tried not to slip in the mud.

"He never cared about anyone, or about what others thought of him. He was the bold one, the one everyone liked." His voice became bitter. "Some in the camp called me Barnaby's brother, and him the younger one."

Something about the way he said it made Jesse think of Eli. Immediately, he felt guilty at the comparison. He had always been jealous of Eli, of his strength and good looks and sense of humor, but they had been friends. Eli had always protected him.

And maybe that's why I resented him.

Jesse shook off the thought. Still, he couldn't help but feel a twinge of sympathy for Tomas.

They sloshed through the camp as quietly as possible, hiding behind a wagon once when they heard someone passing by.

"Here's where I leave you," Tomas said, once they reached the trees at the edge of the camp.

"Don't worry," Parvel said, clapping him on the shoulder. "We'll find your brother." Clearly, he didn't understand this kind of sibling rivalry. Jesse knew that Parvel and his brother had been close.

In fact, that was one of the problems. Parvel was searching for his brother, Justis, who had disappeared five years before. What Parvel didn't know was that Justis now called himself by another name: Captain Demetri.

Jesse and Silas were the only ones who knew. Silas insisted that if they told Parvel, he would do something rash and endanger them all.

"Do you want us to give Barnaby a message from you?" Parvel asked.

Tomas thought about that. "Yes," he said, tightening his cloak against the rain and turning away. "Tell him: don't ever come back."

CHAPTER 5

It was a cold, miserable night for standing watch. Jesse never thought he'd wish they were back in the mountains. *But at least there we could find an overhang or a cave to make camp*, he thought.

Now, after a day of travel, they had reached the soggy, wet terrain of the swamps. Jesse had to content himself with huddling under the draping branches of a tree—a swamp cypress, Silas called it. Jesse had never seen one before. Old Kayne, back in Mir, had taught him to identify all the trees in District One. *He would be fascinated by this place*. The thought made Jesse miss the crusty old hermit.

Kayne would be able to spend days just examining the plants of the swamp. For some reason, when Tomas spoke of the Swamp of the Vanished, Jesse pictured a flat bog with nothing but scum coating the water, like a plowed field after a week's worth of heavy rain.

Instead, the swamp looked more like a forest than anything else. Silas had insisted that they stop as soon as they reached the fringes of the swamp. "It will be safer," he said.

Usually, Jesse would attribute that to Silas' caution, but even Rae wasn't eager to enter the swamp at night. The trees were so tall they seemed to block out the light of the moon, although Jesse knew it was only the heavy storm clouds.

"They say it's the greatest uncharted territory in Amarias."

Even though Jesse recognized Parvel's voice a split second later, he still jumped. Parvel lifted a branch to join Jesse under the tree. His shirt was plastered to him with water, his curly brown hair hung limp around his face, and he had to stoop to keep from hitting his head on the branches of the swamp cypress. He looked like a dripping wet grizzly bear.

"It's not your watch for another hour yet," Jesse said.

"I just couldn't sleep," Parvel replied.

"I'm surprised anyone can in this rain." They were far enough away from the others that Jesse wasn't afraid of waking them. Silas, at least, could sleep through wind, rain, thunderstorms, and possibly an attack by Captain Demetri.

For a moment, Parvel just looked out at the swamp. "Beautiful, isn't it?"

Jesse hadn't thought about it that way before. "I suppose."

"I learned only a bit about the swamps from my tutor. He was rather weak on geography and history, I'm afraid. Mostly had us memorize capitals and trade routes and things of that nature. Terribly dull."

Jesse tried to imagine that kind of life: growing up as the son of a nobleman, with nothing more to do than eat extravagant food and learn about geography. He had learned to read and write and do simple sums at the village school, but that was all.

"Is that where you learned about God?" Jesse asked.

Parvel laughed. "No. In fact, quite the opposite. My tutor was adamantly opposed to any mention of God, even the watered-down talk of the priests. He was also a most miserable man. I decided I did not want to believe as he did, because I did not want to be like him."

"But how do you know so much about God, then?" Jesse asked.

"I made it my goal to find out all I could," Parvel said. "Somehow, I knew that what I heard from the priests couldn't be the truth, or at least not the whole truth. I started a private collection of texts from the Holy Scriptures. Just fragments, you understand. I have yet to find a complete copy."

"Because it's so old?"

"It is old, yes. Preserved from an age no one now remembers. But, more importantly, the king doesn't appreciate the God of the Scriptures. He and his court subscribe to a very different kind of religion."

Instantly, Jesse remembered the dragon sculpture he had seen in Chancellor Doran's parlor. Even thinking about it gave him a sick feeling, like someone was twisting his stomach inside of him.

"I have found many scraps with fire damage on the edges," Parvel said, shaking his head angrily. "I believe they burn all copies of it, Jesse. The most important book in all of history. Can you believe it?"

"I believe it," Jesse said flatly. "We're here in the rain outside a swamp because the king is trying to kill us. It doesn't surprise me that he's willing to burn a few books."

"In any case, God rewards an earnest search for truth. As it says in the Scriptures, 'God did this so that people would seek him and perhaps reach out and find him, though he is not far from any one of us.' I read those words, and ones like them. And I believed."

Jesse turned around, wincing as the rough bark of the tree scraped his neck. He looked toward the camp, where he could dimly see Silas and Rae's sleeping forms. "What about people who don't want to believe?"

"You can only choose for yourself, not for others," Parvel said, shrugging.

He keeps speaking in vague, intellectual terms, like this is a debate in his study at home.

"But what about Rae and Silas?" Jesse asked, getting right to the heart of the matter. "They don't want to listen to anything about God. Silas especially. Rae seems to tolerate it, as if belief in God is a harmless myth. But Silas...."

"Yes, Rae and Silas," Parvel said. He didn't sound upset at all. Instead, he frowned thoughtfully, like Rae and Silas were logic puzzles his tutor would have him solve. "Rae thinks she doesn't need God, that she can do without Him even if He does exist. Silas, on the other hand, doesn't trust God. He doesn't believe that He's good. Besides, he wants revenge for his father's death, and he knows that if God exists, He wouldn't approve of revenge."

That was frustrating to Jesse. "What would it take to change their minds? What more can we *do*?"

"Let me tell you a story," Parvel said, instead of answering. Jesse knew from experience, though, that the story would be the answer.

"Long ago, there was a messenger in the court of King Marias who was sent to the city of Lidia to announce that an army of Westlunders was planning to attack it."

"Who were the Westlunders?" Jesse asked. Parvel often forgot that not everyone was as familiar with history as he was.

"A powerful tribe from the western side of the mountains," Parvel said. "Some even said they were giants. In any case, after hearing the report of the impending attack, the sovereign of Lidia refused to prepare for war. He left the city defenseless and sent the messenger away in disgrace."

"Foolish," Jesse said. "What kind of ruler was he?"

"He believed the city walls were strong enough to withstand any attack," Parvel said, shrugging. "He trusted that faulty belief more than he trusted the messenger. The messenger tried again to gain audience with the sovereign, but he was denied. Three days later, the Westlund army attacked Lidia and put it under siege. After a few months, the city fell and was destroyed."

Jesse didn't try to picture that scene. He had never seen warfare up close, not living in the tiny village of Mir. The war on the Northern Waste was weeks of travel away from District One, and very little news came to them from the battlefield.

"Tell me, Jesse, was it the messenger's fault that the city fell?"

"No," Jesse said immediately. "He did his duty. Even more by going back after he was thrown out of the sovereign's court."

"And that is what you must always remember as a messenger of the truth of God," Parvel said. "You cannot make people accept the truth. You can only present it and pray that God will change their hearts."

Jesse thought about that. "But there's one difference from your story. After the second try, the messenger left. I will get thrown out of the court a hundred times if I need to. I will not give up on Rae and Silas."

"That's the spirit, Jesse." Parvel clapped him on the back, probably harder than he meant to. He often underestimated his own strength. "When they are ready to listen, we will be there."

Jesse nodded. "If we make it out of the swamps alive."

"The Swamps of the Vanished," Parvel mused, stroking his chin. "I wonder what the Westlunders would think of that? It's quite possible they marched across this very ground."

"You mean—" Jesse started.

"Yes. There was once a city in these swamps...Lidia, the very one that fell to the Westlunder army. That was the last Amarias ever heard from these parts. The Lidians simply disappeared."

"Others too, from what I've heard," Jesse added.

Parvel raised a skeptical eyebrow. "And what, exactly, have you heard?"

"Just a few stories," Jesse said quickly, "told by boastful travelers and traders at my aunt and uncle's inn after a bit too much to drink. Probably just lies and exaggerations."

The truth was, he was trying to forget the stories he had heard. None of them ended well. They were tales of noxious bogs, "where just a whiff could poison your blood," not to mention the strange creatures, including dragons. There were men who claimed that they were the only survivors of an expedition to the other side of the swamps, telling how the others in their group disappeared overnight, with most of their possessions left behind.

And they told of giants, ones with matted, greasy hair and fists the size of horse carts. Evil smiles, too, ones that glowed in the darkness of the swamp. The Westlunders, though Jesse had never heard anyone call them by such a polite name.

"They say the giants of the swamp will jump across Amarias in three steps and snatch children from their beds as they go," Parvel said, swooping down and picking Jesse up on the last words.

Jesse kicked him in the shin, laughing. "Put me down, Parvel."

Parvel did. "Isn't that what your nurse told you when you were young?"

"I didn't have a nurse, Parvel," Jesse said, "just a mother and a father."

There it was again. Talk of his parents always made Jesse pull back. But if Parvel noticed, he didn't say anything. Jesse was glad. Even though Parvel was usually right, he didn't want a philosophical answer for why suffering and separation existed. He wanted his parents.

"What is the other squad doing in the swamps, anyway?" Jesse asked, to change the subject.

Parvel frowned in concentration. "You ought to ask Silas to be sure, but I'm fairly certain they are hunting for the fabled city of the giants, a fortress that would put even the proud city of ancient Lidia to shame."

Now Jesse remembered. He had read the entry too. All of them had, though only Silas had memorized all the entries. "In case something happens to the book," he always said.

"The stairs," Jesse said. "There's a staircase in the center of the giants' city that holds the secret to their power. They're looking for the staircase to the sky."

"Imagine it," Parvel said, sweeping his hand toward the stormy sky. "Steps that wind past the tallest of the swamp trees and into the clouds. Perhaps that's how the giants can leap over to District One to steal disobedient children."

"I take it, then, that you don't believe in the Giants' Staircase?"

Parvel shook his head. "No, Jesse. I do not even believe in the giants themselves. Perhaps the Westlunders existed once, but they died out, as many people groups do. They do not live in the swamps."

"How can you be sure?"

"Think about it: an entire civilization, never venturing out of the swamps. One that no one has ever seen. How could they sustain themselves? What would they eat? With whom would they trade?" He shook his head. "No, the Giants' Staircase is just another invention of the king to send a squad of Youth Guard into death."

Jesse looked out at the towering swamp. "Not if we get there first."

Chapter 6

Unlike the stories Jesse had heard at the inn, the Swamp of the Vanished did not have serpents as thick as a barrel, or flesh-eating insects, or mud that reached up and sucked unsuspecting travelers into the heart of the earth.

There were places where mud, rich and thick, collected in pits, but most of the ground was covered with moss, small bushes and a strange matted plant. When Jesse first stepped on it, his feet bounced back slightly. The plant acted as a kind of cushion.

"If we survive this, I am cutting a patch of this and taking it back as a rug," Jesse declared, using his staff to vault himself into the air and letting the matted plant bounce him back.

"We've been walking for eight hours," Silas said. "Haven't you gotten tired of that yet?"

Jesse bounced again. "No. How could anyone get tired of this?"

Rae smiled a little. Jesse had caught her taking a few bounces herself. Never when Silas was looking, though.

She's probably afraid he'll laugh at her too. Well, I don't care. It's been too long since I've had any fun.

Occasionally, Rae would pull out her dagger and slice away the thin, stringy vines hanging from the trees, but Jesse knew it was just to keep herself occupied. For every plant that Rae took out of their path, there were a thousand more. Jesse felt almost as if the trees and undergrowth were closing in around them, trying to suffocate them.

Well, let them try, he said. *Rae and her mighty sword will attack them and drive them back.* It was a funny thought, picturing Rae in a suit of armor doing battle with weeds. He laughed out loud.

And he ran into Silas, who had stopped without warning. "What?" Jesse demanded, trying to peer over Silas' shoulder. "Did you find a giant?"

"I don't know what it is," Silas said. They gathered around Silas' discovery. There, half-hidden in the weeds, was a glint of metal.

Parvel pushed away the plants to reveal a thin piece of metal that gleamed a dull gold. The scrolls and engraved designs outlined a perfect triangle.

"It's a weapon," Rae said.

"Rae, to you, anything shiny is a weapon," Jesse said, grinning.

She picked it up and shoved it toward Jesse. "See that point? It's as sharp as a blade."

"Which is exactly why you should set it back down," Parvel said, guiding Rae's arm away from Jesse's face. Jesse shot him a look of gratitude.

"It's perfectly even," Silas said. "The blacksmith who made it must have been a master." He ran a finger along the base. "It looks like it was once connected to something."

"That's because it's a weapon," Rae insisted.

But that didn't seem right to Jesse. The triangle was too wide. Weapons like knives and arrows came to a narrow point. This was more like the blade of a miniature plow than anything else. But that wouldn't explain the ornate design.

"It's a sundial," Jesse finally said, "the point of one, anyway."

"I think you might have something there," Silas said. "It does look like it was broken off of a base."

"No," Parvel said, taking it from Rae. "No, it can't be. The angle is wrong. Very wrong."

"He knows the angle of the sun," Rae muttered. "Of *course* he does."

"For it to accurately measure time, the top would have to be *here*," Parvel said, indicating the angle with his hand.

But Rae had already wandered off. "If it's not a weapon, I'm not interested."

"Maybe whoever left this here misjudged the angle," Silas suggested.

"If it were a crude, handmade dial, perhaps, but this is a work of art," Parvel said. He studied it some more, turning it over in his hands. "No, this does not measure the height of the sun."

Jesse thought about all the things that could be measured—rainfall, temperature, crop growth—none of them seemed to fit.

"Look at those designs," Parvel said, shaking his head in wonder. "They're so detailed. How was it done?"

"They probably poured it into a mold," Jesse guessed. That, he knew, was the easiest way to create a detailed design.

Silas shook his head, running a finger over the flat surface of the dial. "You can feel the hammer marks. This was cut out of a sheet of metal. I've never seen anything like it."

Jesse tested it himself. Sure enough, he could feel tiny grooves and indentations in the surface of the triangular dial.

"Before I joined the Guard, I was apprenticed to a blacksmith," Silas explained. "A very poor one, in fact, but it was a trade. He didn't want to let me break my indenture contract to join the Guard, but the Patrol soon changed his mind on that."

Jesse looked at the dial again. "What is this doing here anyway, in the middle of the swamp?"

"I think I could answer that," Rae's voice called from a distance away. Jesse could see a smirk on her face. "While you men were busy examining your chunk of metal, I found the rest of the city."

Even Parvel jerked his head up at that. "The—" His voiced trailed off. "No, it can't be. It was destroyed so long ago...." He took the dial with him as they went to investigate.

"It's not a functioning city," Rae said. "At least, not unless the citizens like their buildings in ruins."

Past the thick trees was a clearing that gently sloped up a hill. On top of the hill were the broken walls of an ancient city. "The ruins of Lidia," Parvel breathed. "It *does* exist!"

Jutting out from the ruins, in what looked like the center

of the city was a huge tree, the largest Jesse had ever seen. Even at a distance, it was impressive. *You can probably see its crown from the outskirts of the swamp*.

Rae was the first to run forward, but Silas remained planted where he was. "I say we leave it be," he said. "We have to find the other squad. It's our mission."

Parvel looked almost pained, like someone had destroyed his most valuable possession in front of him.

"Maybe the other squad is living in the ruins," Jesse suggested, although he didn't think it was likely. "Maybe that's how they escaped the Patrol for so long."

It wasn't a very reasonable answer, but Silas didn't protest any more. *He wants to explore just as much as we do*, Jesse guessed.

There was something mysterious about the ruins, something that drew Jesse toward them. Even the air around them felt old, somehow.

That feeling only grew once they climbed the hill and entered the city. There was no need to find a gate. Hardly any section of the wall came above Jesse's head, though, from the amount of crumbled stone on the ground, the wall had once been very impressive.

Once over the walls, Jesse could hardly decide where to look. Even though much of the city was damaged, he could tell that Lidia had once been a marvel of architecture.

"Parvel," Silas called from underneath a partially crumbled archway, "before you go off hunting antiques, I think there's something you should see."

Although perfectly calm, as usual, Silas' voice was serious

enough that Jesse hurried over. Past the archway and down three steps was a sunken courtyard, vines and moss covering the stones.

What was more interesting, though, was the camp that was set up in the corner: a firepit and a mat, kept from blowing away by a sword and a leather pack that lay on it.

Someone else is here.

They stared at the camp for a few seconds. Then Jesse headed for the steps. "That's it. We're leaving."

"Wait," Rae said, moving closer. "This might belong to the other Youth Guard squad. No need to assume it's an enemy."

"One person? Alone?" Jesse challenged her. "Silas, weren't all of the members of this squad alive and together?"

Silas closed his eyes, as he always did when recalling an entry from the Forbidden Book. "Yes. The last report, though, was given nearly ten days ago now. Anything could have happened since then."

Jesse thought about that. What would it be like to be the only one of your squad left, alone and abandoned in a ruined city with a trained killer after you?

Rae picked up the sword on the mat, drawing it out of its sheath. It was a long broadsword, and her small arm strained to lift it. "Why did he leave behind a weapon?"

Jesse gave the first answer he could think of. "Because he vanished. Just like all the legends say."

"That's not possible," Silas scoffed.

"Perhaps not," Parvel said, "but something is wrong here." He bent down and began looking through the leather pack.

"Regardless, I agree with Jesse's first reaction," Silas said.

"We should leave here immediately. This person could come back at any time, and we don't know if we would face a friend or an enemy."

"Wait," Parvel said, raising a hand. "I doubt our mysterious figure will return any time soon. There hasn't been anyone here for a long time. Look at the fire. No ash, just a few charred sticks. Everything else has been blown away."

"The rain last night could have washed that away. He could still be back tonight." Silas glanced up. "And the sun will go down soon."

"It's not just that. The sword has rust on the blade," Parvel said, nodding toward it. He held up a cloth bundle that, when unwrapped, revealed biscuits, green with mold. "Even the hardtack spoiled. That takes days, even weeks."

Jesse saw something glinting underneath the mat. He knelt down and picked it up.

It was a golden medallion, heavy in Jesse's hand, the symbol of Amarias stamped in the center. He held it closer. Around the edge of the medallion, forming a circle, was a serpent-like dragon. Quickly, he dropped it. It was the same style of dragon as the one he had seen in Chancellor Doran's parlor, the one with eyes that seemed to stare at him.

"This wasn't a Youth Guard camp," Jesse said firmly. He pointed to the medallion.

Silas picked it up and examined the front. It didn't seem to alarm him at all. Then he turned it over. "There's an inscription," he said. "*Guard Rider*. That's what the Forbidden Book calls the king's assassins."

"This camp was abandoned," Parvel said solemnly.

"Whoever slept here left and never came back."

"No," Rae said. "The sword and pack would be gone if that were the case, and the mat rolled up. It looks to me like someone was *here* when they disappeared. Sleeping, maybe."

"But there's no blood," Silas said, "no signs of struggle. It isn't possible."

Rae shrugged. "I'm just telling you what it looks like."

"What do you suggest we do next?" Silas asked, looking to Parvel, their captain.

"Search the city," Parvel said. "Look for a source of food—there's a reason this Guard Rider camped here—and check for signs of danger. We must be sure we are safe before the sun sets."

Rae disappeared almost immediately, climbing up a pile of rubble that made Jesse dizzy to even look at. *Probably looking for the armory*, Jesse decided. He soon lost sight of Silas too.

Parvel, on the other hand, barely got three steps away from the camp before he stopped, taking in the ruins around him. "It's smaller than I expected," he muttered. "Hardly more than four hundred could have lived here." He looked a bit like a madman, hurrying from place to place, still clutching the golden dial and exclaiming to himself.

Jesse had seen ruins before, of the underground city of Urad. But those had been simple huts and mining shafts. This was something entirely different. Every building seemed like a palace. Outside the small courtyard was a larger one, with stone steps leading up to a porch, the roof still intact. Everywhere Jesse turned, he saw scrolling designs on bits of

brick, intricate metal gates and broken pillars that must have stretched up to four stories when they were still intact.

Jesse even found a kind of vineyard with small fruit, tangled around trellises, even though the Lidian harvesters were long gone. The sickly yellow shade of the plants made them look poisonous, but clearly the plants had once been cultivated for food. Jesse picked one and took a small bite of it.

It had a stringy texture, but tasted mildly sweet. Jesse decided that he liked it. Besides, that morning they had run out of the small spice cakes Margo had given them, and he was hungry.

The vineyard led to a large, pillared platform, where Parvel was pacing around, saying something about imported jade and circumferences.

"Find anything?" Jesse asked.

Parvel looked up. "It's dead," he said, looking very solemn.

Jesse stared at him. "What's dead?"

He pointed to the tree in the center of the city, just a short distance from the courtyard. This close, Jesse was struck by its impressive height, but sure enough, the bare branches were a sickly gray.

"I don't know how it happened," Parvel said, shaking his head. "A tree that large couldn't dry up. Its roots must go very deep, and the swamp seems to make every living thing thrive."

"Maybe it's a disease, a blight," Jesse suggested. For some reason, the pale tree made him nervous, like it was a ghostly guard towering over the ruins of Lidia. He looked away.

A flash of color caught Jesse's eye. He walked to the center of the courtyard, where blue-green tiles formed a pattern that seemed to illustrate the phases of the moon. "What a strange design," Jesse said. Then he realized he was starting to act like Parvel, talking to himself.

Lidia had been a proud city, Jesse decided. A marvel of architecture, the most advanced of its day, most likely. *But now it's in ruins, like any other ancient, conquered city.*

"Why did they build here?" he asked Parvel. It took Parvel a minute to realize that Jesse was talking to him and another few second to pull his eyes away from the ruins.

"Lidia was a center for agriculture in this region," Parvel said. "No crops can be grown near the mountains, for obvious reasons. These lowlands, though, were perfect for growing rice. That was what gave the city its wealth from the dawn of the kingdom and even before."

Then he hurried off, probably to explore a fascinating ancient carving.

"Rice," Jesse said thoughtfully. "I wonder if it's still growing somewhere." He shook his head. "Stop it. There's no one to talk to here."

If I were a rice field, where would I be? Parvel had called them the lowlands. Jesse wandered over to the west side of the ruins and climbed outside the city wall. When it came to physical strength, Jesse fell behind his squad members, but he knew how to use his mind. *I can find food for us*, he thought. *I always do.*

The grade on this side was steeper, and he almost fell

down headfirst. Only a quick stab at the ground with his staff saved him.

Jesse studied the ground beneath him. Actually, he wasn't sure what rice plants looked like. He'd only seen rice once before, when a merchant staying at the inn had showed him a sack. It was a rare delicacy. "Can only be grown in a few places in the kingdom," the merchant had said.

Suddenly, Jesse jerked his head up, scanning the thick growth of trees in front of him. He had seen something move. He was sure of it. Something big.

Now, though, everything was still. A few frogs croaked, and somewhere, a bird crowed. *That's what I saw*, Jesse told himself. *Just a bird. A...very large bird.*

Still, he kept his eyes up, glancing down only occasionally to look for a rice field. The ruins had done strange things to his nerves. *The idea that a man could disappear from his camp without warning, without leaving a trace of explanation behind....*

It took Jesse a second to realize that he was falling. The dirt had crumbled under his feet, and he slid down into a pit.

He was still getting his balance from the fall when he realized something else. He hadn't landed on solid ground – he was sinking. The swamp was pulling him under.

"Help!" he sputtered, trying to pull his legs out of...mud? No, it was thicker and darker than mud, nearly up to his waist. *Tar.*

Jesse thrashed around, trying to work himself over to the bank. He only managed to twist himself in the other direction. Now that it had him, the tar wasn't about to let go.

Even pushing down with his staff didn't help. The bottom of the pit either didn't exist, or it was made out of sand and mud, not solid enough to push off of. The tar held Jesse fast, and soon he gave up, exhausted, and faced the ruins on the hill. "Silas! Rae! Parvel!"

There was no answer.

Chapter 7

How humiliating, Jesse thought, staring at the ruins. He had shouted until he was hoarse. *Silas, Rae, and Parvel must have heard. They'll be here soon.*

He knew exactly what would happen when they arrived. Parvel would laugh first, tossing out a few of his good-natured insults. Rae would smirk the whole time they rescued him. Silas would scan the area, come up with a plan and then tell him not to go off on his own again. And all of them would tease him about it until the day he died.

Well, it can't be helped, Jesse thought, sighing loudly. *There's no way out of here on my own.*

He resolved to wait. He couldn't even lean against his staff; when he tried, the added weight only made it sink deeper into the pit. All he could do was stand there. The tar, warmed by hours in the sun, had started to feel like a comfortable blanket. It wasn't an uncomfortable wait.

But no one came. There was no call from inside the city, no movement on the battlements, no figure running down the hill toward the swamps. Now Jesse began to worry. *What if they made camp on the other side of the city? My voice can't carry that far. But they'll come looking for me when they realize I'm missing...won't they?*

The fear of being left in the swamp all night made Jesse struggle against the tar pit again, stopping his thrashing and kicking to shout for help every now and then.

I should never have left, he repeated over and over. *Should never have gone off on my own. Why do I always try to be the hero?*

"Hello down there," a cheerful voice behind him called. It wasn't Silas, Parvel or Rae. Jesse was sure of it. He craned his head around, which was easier than trying to move his whole body.

The person on the bank was little more than a boy, with flaming red hair that looked like someone had set it on fire. He knelt on the ground, reaching his arm toward Jesse. "You're just out of reach," he said. "That's too bad. I was hoping this would be easy."

"Who are you?" Jesse demanded. He doubted someone so young would be an enemy, but he had learned from Silas that it never hurt to be cautious.

"My name's Owen," the boy said.

Somewhere in the back of his mind, Jesse knew that name sounded familiar. *The Book. He's one of the members of the missing squad! But where are the others?*

As exciting as the realization was, there was a more important question to ask. "Can you get me out of here?"

"Don't know," Owen said, cocking his head slightly. "But I

can sure try." He frowned, reaching down and sticking his finger in the tar. "Your clothes are going to be ruined, though."

"My mother always told me not to play in the swamp tar pits in my good clothes," Jesse said dryly.

Owen laughed out loud. "You're funny."

At the moment, Jesse didn't feel funny—more like hot, tired, and sticky—but he didn't argue.

"Now, if I can just find a rope or a stick..." Owen said, looking around.

"I have a stick!" Jesse said. It took a mighty yank, but he managed to pull his staff out of the tar and wave it in the air.

Owen paused. "That's nice. You practically rescue yourself." He lay down on the ground near the pit. "So you don't pull *me* in," he explained. "That would be a little messy. All right, I'm going to pull you over to the bank, then up and out."

Jesse made sure to hold the end with the knob, to give himself a better grip. Owen took the other end and gave it a good yank. For such a small fellow, he had a strong pull. Still, Jesse barely moved forward. The tar didn't want to give up its prisoner.

"Awful sticky, this stuff," Owen said, almost apologetically. "The muck of doom, I call it." He gave the staff another yank. This time Jesse barely managed to hang on to his staff, and still he was too far away from the edge.

"Owen!" a distant voice called. A girl's voice.

Owen closed his eyes and muttered something to himself. "They're coming," he said to Jesse, a look of dread on his face.

"I'm in a tar pit," Jesse pointed out. "How much worse could it be?" Even his voice sounded squeezed and forced after the exertion of fighting the tar.

"You haven't met Nero and Talia," Owen said in a low tone. "Sure you don't want to duck under that tar for a bit?"

Jesse shook his head, one part of his body he could still move easily.

Owen shrugged. "Suit yourself." He raised his voice. "Nero! Talia! Give me a hand, will you?"

Jesse had a suspicion that he was going to meet the other missing squad members. *But there are only three. Don't all squads have four members?*

Two sets of footsteps, soft against the moss. The newcomers came from behind Jesse, so he couldn't see them. He knew it would be too much work to turn. "Owen, what—" a girl's voice started.

Jesse realized he was not making a good first impression. "Let me explain," he said, trying to focus his tired mind enough to come up with an explanation. "I—"

"Who are you?" a strong male voice demanded, interrupting him.

Jesse decided to attract their attention right away. "Jesse. I've come to rescue you."

Silence. "Are you sure you have that right?" Owen asked. "Because we're just fine. You're the one in trouble."

Jesse just closed his eyes, trying to figure out how to explain. *If only he knew.*

"I don't trust him. How do you know he won't kill us once we get him out?" the girl – Talia? – pointed out. "Or lead someone to us? He knows where we are now."

Jesse fought a growing frustration. "We're here to rescue you, not kill you!"

"Explain yourself," Nero ordered. It seemed like everything he said was an order. "Quickly."

Jesse tried to think. This was not how he pictured their meeting with the missing squad. Besides, his head felt like it was full of the tar around him. "Parvel got sick, so I went into the desert...and we were almost executed...a Patrol captain is chasing us...and we went into the mountains with the dwarves...before escaping the Rebellion...and finding the Forbidden Book...."

He trailed off. *I must sound like a madman.* "It's a long story," he finished weakly. "Several long stories, actually."

"Parvel," Talia muttered. "Silas and Rae are in his squad, aren't they?"

Something about the way Talia said their names made Jesse want to deny it. "Yes?"

"Excellent," Owen muttered, still flopped on the ground, almost at eye level with Jesse. "You had to bring *them* up, didn't you?"

"I should have known," Talia said. "They always taunted us during training. Said that we'd fail in our quest. Rae especially. You say the others are nearby?"

"Yes," Jesse said, "in the ruins." Something caught his eye, over in the sand of the tar pit bank. *Odd. Was that...?*

No. Your imagination. That's all. But Jesse wasn't sure that it was. For a moment, he thought he had seen something moving in the sand of the bank.

"Then let them find you." Talia's voice got more distant. *She's walking away.* "I say we—"

The movement again, this time sending a trickle of sand down into the tar in front of Jesse. "There's something in the bank," Jesse said, trying not to panic.

"Don't interrupt," Talia said coolly.

"No, there's something alive," Jesse said, trying to back away from...whatever it was. He didn't care if it would make him sink deeper into the tar. "In the bank."

Owen winced. "Not good, not good." He looked up. "You two, get back over here and help me haul him up." No movement. "Now!"

Apparently Owen, unlike Nero, didn't give orders very often, because Talia and Nero came over and grabbed on to the end of the staff. The force of the pull nearly tore Jesse's arms out, but he held on.

He let go with one hand and grabbed at the edge of the bank, tearing away mossy plants. "Stop it," Owen shouted. He threw Jesse's staff on the ground. "Let us pull you."

The sound of more sand falling, then something like a hiss. "Pull fast!" he yelled back.

Two pairs of arms grabbed him and the tar pit surrendered. Nero and Owen helped Jesse away from the edge.

"Watch yourselves." Talia's voice. When Jesse looked up, he saw a girl aiming an arrow...right at him.

He gasped and rolled to the side. Talia let go...and shot into the pit. "I think I got it," she said, leaning over to look.

Jesse peered back into the tar pit. There, floating on the surface was what looked like a long, flat lizard, with strange webbed feet splayed in either direction.

Owen reached in for it, lying down on the bank's edge again.

"Get your hand out of there," Nero commanded.

"It's dead, Captain," Owen said sarcastically. "What's it going to do, slime me to death?"

He pulled the creature out of the pit, holding onto the arrow. "A tar-strider," he said, displaying the stabbed creature like a trophy. "That's what Barnaby called it, anyway. They're kind of poisonous."

"Kind of?" Jesse asked.

Owen shrugged. "Well, one bit Nero a few weeks ago, but after Barnaby sucked the poison out, he only just swelled up for a few days. And got a rash. And had a fever."

"Well, if that's all, why don't we find one and keep it for a pet?" Jesse asked, rolling his eyes.

Owen's face lit up. "That's what *I* said." He turned to Nero. "See? You said I was the only one stupid enough to suggest something like that." He looked down at the tar-strider. "Hey, do you think we could eat these?"

But Talia, at least, wasn't watching Owen and the tar-strider. She was staring right at Jesse, like he might bolt into the swamp or draw a sword and stab her.

Jesse stood, his sticky clothes peeling apart slowly, and stared at his three rescuers, trying to match them to the pictures in the Forbidden Book.

Talia wore a full-length dress, longer than the tunics that Rae often wore, and her blonde hair fell down her back in a thick braid. But her hawk-like eyes and stern glare refused to let Jesse think of her as a girl content to sit around and embroider pillows.

Nero was even more intimidating, with close-cut brown hair, heavy eyebrows and broad shoulders. The oldest, probably. Certainly the strongest.

It was strange, recognizing their faces when he had never seen them in person before. The court artists who had sketched them for the Book had done a remarkable job, recreating every feature to the smallest detail.

But there were only three, and Jesse knew who was missing. "Where's Barnaby?" he asked.

Immediately, Nero's eyes narrowed. "How did you know about Barnaby?" he demanded.

"Maybe he's a spy," Talia said, "sent by the Rebellion to kill the kings' Youth Guard."

Jesse started to protest, but Nero interrupted him. "This is no member of the Rebellion," he said, sounding disgusted. "Look at him! He can barely walk."

"I need to talk to you," Jesse insisted. "You're in great danger."

"We saved your life," Nero said, turning away. "Now, leave us be, or it will be the worse for you."

He and Talia began to walk into the swamp.

"We're leaving him?" Owen protested. He ran to catch up, waving the tar-strider in their direction. For a moment, Jesse was afraid it was going to go sailing off the arrow and hit Talia in the head. Thankfully for Owen, the arrow held.

They don't believe me, Jesse realized. *They think I'm crazy. Or lying.*

He also knew he couldn't give up. This was a matter of life or death.

Jesse struggled to his feet and grabbed the tar-encrusted staff. "You don't understand," he shouted after them. This time, he was careful to watch for pits. "The king is trying to kill you!"

At that, Talia hesitated, but Nero kept walking. "That's impossible. Don't listen to him. He's trying to get us to abandon our mission."

"No," Jesse insisted. "I saw your names in a book. I saw the assassin's camp in the ruins."

"I don't see any book," Nero said. "I've never seen any assassin, and we've been in these parts for weeks now."

"You know what I think," Talia said, green eyes squinting at Jesse in hatred. "Rae and Silas aren't here at all. They sent him here. To follow us."

"That's the most ridiculous thing I've ever heard," Jesse blurted.

Wrong thing to say. Talia stiffened. "They should have at least come up with a better story. The king determined to kill us! Why, even telling such a lie is treason."

Jesse gritted his teeth and tried to remember that he had thought much the same when he'd first heard the truth about the Youth Guard. *But at least I was willing to listen to reason.*

"Go back to those who sent you," Nero said, and his voice sounded like a final judgment. He glanced down at Jesse's crippled leg. "You don't belong here."

Jesse felt his face grow hot under the layers of tar. In Nero's voice, he heard the taunts of every schoolyard bully, every leering beggar who had reminded him of his crippled leg.

He *did* belong here. He had survived a sandstorm, assassins, a cave-in and a fall into a rushing river. He had kept going when others would have turned back, risked his life for his squad members when others would have let them go. *I am a Youth Guard member as much as any of them, and probably a better one too.*

Jesse opened his mouth to tell Nero all this, but nothing came out. Anger had taken his voice away.

"Come on, Owen," Nero commanded.

"Actually, no," Owen said, stepping away from them. "I side with the crazy tar-covered boy."

"Really?" Jesse blurted.

Owen gave him a withering look. "You're not exactly helping my case."

"Fine," Nero said, quickly recovering from a look of shock. "Talia and I will continue without you."

"And the reward for a completed mission will be ours without you," Talia added.

"Happy for you," Owen said, waving. "Let me know where that Giants' Staircase led to, eh?"

Talia shot him one last dirty look before she and Nero disappeared into the thickets of the deep swamp.

"That was your squad," Jesse said, staring at the redhead in disbelief. "You can't just *leave* them."

"What do you mean? I've been looking for an excuse to get rid of them for weeks now," Owen said, waving him away. He held up the arrow. It was empty. "Slipped the tar-strider into Talia's pack when she wasn't looking," he confessed, grinning. "Too bad I won't be there to see her reaction."

Jesse didn't think it was too bad. In fact, he hoped Nero and Talia would be far, far away by the time that happened. *But I doubt they will be.* The sun was already setting. In another quarter of an hour, it would be too dark to travel far. *Unless Nero and Talia want to chance the Swamps of the Vanished at night.*

He looked back at the tar pit, a distance away and hoped, for their sake, they wouldn't be so foolish.

"That was some story you were telling," Owen said cheerfully, sticking the arrow into a colorfully woven bag on his back. The tip poked out dangerously. "How did you come up with it?"

"Easy," Jesse said flatly. "It's true. The king is trying to kill the Youth Guard."

Owen stopped and stared at him. "You don't have to keep it up, you know. As long as you're headed out of here, I won't leave you by yourself."

"There's nothing to keep up," Jesse said, feeling like he was endlessly repeating himself. "It's true."

"But you're not in the Guard," Owen said. "At least, I don't recognize you from the training camp."

He seemed to be waiting for a response. "That's part of the long story I told you about," Jesse said, not sure how to summarize a month's worth of adventure in a few sentences. "But, I tell you, you're in danger. You and your squad need to leave here."

"I'm all for that," Owen said, shrugging. "I'm through with this madness. We've been here for weeks now, barely finding enough food and clean water to stay alive. Searched the whole swampland three times without any sign of a giant or a giant civilization. Ever since Barnaby disappeared—"

Jesse's hand automatically went to the token around his neck. It was still there, tar pit and all. "What happened to him?"

There was no trace of Owen's grin now. "We don't know. That's the worst of it. He left to gather fruit from the orchard early one morning just before dawn, and he...never came back."

Jesse swallowed hard. "That seems to be the theme in these swamps."

"And his bird too," Owen added. "I think Barnaby left and went back to his family. They live near the swamps, you know. That's what kept us alive for so long—Barnaby knew things about the swamp. What to eat, how to make shelters, all that."

That was good. Jesse hoped Owen had paid attention to Barnaby's lessons. They might need that information. Then he started thinking about what Owen had said about Barnaby's disappearance.

"Like I said," Owen continued, "this mission of ours is pointless. Giants, they said. A staircase, they said. What kind of crazy—"

"Did you say Barnaby was in an orchard?" Jesse asked. "An orchard back in the ruins of Lidia?"

Owen stopped, blinked at the sudden change in subject.

"Yes. There were several in different parts of the city that he—"

"What time of day was it?"

Owen squinted at Jesse. "You know, you have a bad habit of interrupting people when they're talking."

That didn't seem particularly important to Jesse at the moment. "Owen. Was it night when Barnaby disappeared?"

"Yes," Owen said. "Just before dawn, anyway. But what—"

Jesse was already running back up the hill, toward the ruins. Barnaby had disappeared at night looking for food in the city. The Guard Rider had probably disappeared during the night while making camp in the city.

Parvel, Silas and Rae were all in the city. And night had fallen.

CHAPTER 8

There was no one in the city.

As soon as he stumbled over the city walls, Jesse half expected Silas to scold him for leaving the ruins, Rae to laugh at his tar-covered clothes and Parvel to lead him to a rare mural he had uncovered. But none of them did.

We have to find them, Jesse thought, his panic growing every time he and Owen turned onto a new street and saw no one.

On the way up the hill, through the growing fog, Owen had peppered Jesse with questions, but now, in the city, they moved silently, pressing themselves against crumbling walls and ducking under old archways, always keeping their backs to the wall, always looking for something, anything.

Jesse wasn't sure if he should call for Parvel, Silas and Rae. *What if they're making camp on the outskirts of the city or in the swamp somewhere? Or what if they're looking for me?*

Or what if someone else is looking for me…but for a different reason?

They wandered through a street that looked like it had

once been the home of a bustling marketplace. The moonlight, reflecting off the white stone, was their only light. *At least here there aren't any tar pits to fall into*, Jesse thought.

"Let's go up higher," Owen said, louder than he should have. Some of the buildings had two stories, with pillared porches jutting out over the street. Jesse examined them doubtfully. A few looked like they might fall apart and crumble into dust. Some already had.

But Owen was already inside one of the buildings, a blacksmith's shop, judging by the large brick oven inside. He darted up the staircase at the back of the shop.

"Slow down," Jesse grumbled, leaning heavily on his staff as he limped up the steps.

"You're like an old man with a cane," Owen said, laughing.

Right then, Jesse wanted to act like an old man and hit him with his "cane." "I'm fifteen, only one or two years older than you. You're just faster."

"You're more than two years older than me," Owen said, a mischievous grin appearing on his face. "Promise you won't tell anyone?"

Jesse gestured around to the moonlit ruins. "Who, exactly, do you think I'm going to tell?"

"Good point," Owen admitted. "I'm eleven and a half." He kept going up the stairs. "Told the Patrol at the muster that I was thirteen."

"And he believed you?"

"I don't think he cared very much."

Owen had a point. Most Patrol didn't care about anything other than getting paid.

They had reached a landing that led out to the balcony porch. "Watch yourself," Jesse warned as Owen scampered over to the low railing at the far end of the porch. Jesse hung back a few steps, ready to lunge forward and grab him if anything started to crack or groan under their weight.

Jesse scanned the intersecting streets. No movement, no light from a fire, no signs of life at all. Just the mist slowly seeping into the ruins from the swamp below.

"Anyone here?" Owen shouted down into the empty street.

With strength he didn't know he had, Jesse jumped forward and pulled Owen back. "What are you doing?" he demanded. "You're going to get us both killed."

"If you're so worried about danger, let's just leave," Owen said, not sounding alarmed by Jesse's outburst. "Spend the night somewhere else and come back in the morning."

Jesse felt his heart rate increasing. Panic flooded his body. *Where are they? They have to be here. They have to be.* "I have to find them, Owen. You don't understand."

"Calm down. They're probably just on the other side of the city." But even he sounded doubtful.

"I will *not* calm down!" Dimly, Jesse realized he was shouting, but he didn't care. "The last time people I loved disappeared, I never saw them again."

There was a pause for a moment. Then Owen ventured timidly, "Who?"

"My parents." It hurt even to say it.

"Oh," Owen shrugged. "Maybe they got stolen by the giants too. Or maybe they just didn't want to come back."

For one insane moment, Jesse wanted to strike out at him,

push him over the side of the balcony, for talking about his parents like that as if they didn't matter. But he was frozen with rage, unable to move.

Jesse blinked. His hands were knotted in fists. Slowly, he loosened them, shame washing over him. *I could have killed him*, Jesse realized, stunned.

Back in Mir, he would sometimes let his temper get the better of him, especially when someone was taunting him because of his crippled leg. Now, though, he was a believer in God, a Christian. He hadn't expected to still get angry…and never like this. *God, forgive me*, he prayed.

Deep down inside, he knew why Owen's comment had made him so angry. There were those old doubts, coming up again like they had in the long nights right after his parents disappeared. *What if Owen is right? What if they really didn't want to take care of me anymore? What if they moved on to a better life…without me?*

Owen was still looking out over the city, not even realizing the impact his careless comment was having on Jesse. *He's only eleven*, Jesse reminded himself. *He doesn't know any better.*

"Well, no one's there, as far as I can see," Owen said, turning. "How about we search again in the morning, eh?" He snapped his fingers and started down the stairs. "And I know just the place to spend the night."

Jesse followed without protest. He suddenly realized how tired he was. *Maybe Owen is right. We can't do anything more until morning.*

"Where are we going?" he asked, once they had gotten down to the street.

"Somewhere I found when my squad first got here," Owen said, never turning around. "Don't worry, it's about the safest place we could find."

That wasn't very comforting. Everything about the city gave Jesse the sense that nothing within its walls was safe. The distant croaking of frogs in the swamps was the only sound, and their footsteps the only movement. Not even a breeze made its way through the thick forest that surrounded the city. It was as if the city itself, once alive and thriving, was silent in the grave.

"Look," Jesse said, pointing to a grate in the street. Something wispy seemed to be coming out of it. "Is that… smoke?"

Owen studied it for a second. "It's just the fog," he said, "a trick of the light."

The way he said it so confidently, Jesse almost believed him. But some nagging voice told him that the wisps looked exactly like ghosts coming into the ruins. *That's impossible*, he told himself. *Ghosts don't exist.*

After a few streets, Jesse lost all sense of direction, but Owen moved confidently, pausing only a few times to glance back at the towering tree in the center of the city. Finally, Owen stopped in front of a thick wall decorated with spikes. "Climb over," he said.

Jesse stared at the spikes. "No thank you."

Owen laughed. "Just kidding." He turned the corner and pointed. The wall, spikes and all, must have been hit with a battering ram the likes of which Jesse had never seen, because boulders were scattered about like they were no more than a child's set of clay blocks.

Jesse scrambled over the rocks, using his staff to keep his balance. Even though they started at the same time, Owen was waiting impatiently for him at the bottom. *He could probably best Rae with his climbing skills.*

Thinking about Rae made Jesse worry again, so he pushed the thought aside. *In the morning. We'll find them in the morning.*

Inside the wall was a round tower, rather small compared to the size and strength of the gate. "In here," Owen said, slipping inside the archway. The door had rotted away, or been broken down, long ago.

It took a few seconds for Jesse's eyes to adjust to the even deeper darkness. The only light came from three windows, complete and unbroken, made of bits of colored glass. They were placed at equal distances from each other, set deep in the thick walls of the circular room.

A dark figure stood in front of each.

Jesse almost gasped before he realized the figures were statues, stiff and unmoving.

A sharp crack split the silence. Jesse jerked his head to see Owen striking flint and lighting a torch. The light cut through the darkness, showing more features of the room: a tiled floor, a huge golden chandelier with partially melted candles and a staircase at the back of the hall.

Owen joined Jesse in the middle of the room, casting strange shadows with the torch. Jesse glanced down at the floor beneath him. In the tiles was a blue circle with three intertwined silver *S's. Strange that a city would have its own coat of arms. But then, this place is like no city I've ever seen.*

"This must have been a fortress or a citadel of some kind," Jesse said, more to fill the silence than anything else. "A last line of defense."

Owen shrugged. "Whatever it was, it has beds upstairs. Nero and Talia said we couldn't stay and that we needed to accomplish our mission, blah, blah, blah. So we traveled around the swamps and slept on the ground." He started to head for the staircase.

Jesse stopped him, pointing to the statues. "Who are they?"

"Probably the people who lived here."

It was obvious from his tone that Owen didn't care, but he followed Jesse to the first statue. *Probably doesn't want to be left alone in the dark any more than I do.*

The first was an imposing figure, a man with straight, even features, every detail on his stone robe etched to perfection. He was very tall, so tall that Jesse thought his height must be exaggerated for effect. A circlet rested on his high, noble forehead.

"Jardos, Sovereign of Lidia," Owen said.

"How did you know that?" Jesse asked.

"I may only be eleven, but I can read." Owen pointed to the base of the statue.

Jesse knelt down. Sure enough, there was an inscription in the stone. "Bring the light closer, please."

Beneath what Owen had read was a poem in perfectly carved letters:

High was my reach,
Strong was my will.
Still do I rule,
Though I lie still.
Forever mine
The noble hill.

"He must have been the ruler of Lidia," Jesse said.

"That would explain the crown," Owen said, yawning.

For once, Jesse moved faster than the younger Youth Guard member, following the curve of the tower wall to the next statue. Owen trudged over, dutifully holding up the torch so Jesse could see the second figure.

Compared to Jardos, this man seemed insignificant. He had no hair and stooped over, plain clothes sagging around him and a book in his withered hands. Still, there was something important about him, not in his bearing, but in his eyes. Where Jardos' eyes had seemed proud and noble, this man's were quiet and wise.

Hyram, Scholar of Lidia, the inscription read. Then, beneath it, another rhyme.

The toast of all
The seers and sages,
I sought to live
Within the pages,
Preserve the past
For future ages.

"Why would they make a statue of a stuffy teacher?" Owen muttered, making a face. "He even looks like the school master back home: old and boring."

"Don't be disrespectful," Jesse said.

Owen looked at him in disbelief. "He's *dead*!"

Jesse sighed. "That's *why* you should be respectful."

"So, I can be disrespectful to living people, but I'm not allowed to say anything bad about dead people?" Owen demanded, incredulous.

Ignoring him, Jesse moved on to the third statue. He liked the fact that the Lidians had honored Hyram, someone who wasn't strong or powerful, but who had clearly done great things for the city.

Owen flashed the torch's light on the third statue and started to back away. "Okay, there they are. All three. Now can we get some sleep?" But Jesse was already reading the inscription, "Vincent, Shipbuilder of Lidia."

Something about the name must have made Owen curious, because the torchlight stopped, then moved closer. Jesse looked up at the statue. A strong man with powerful arms held a scroll of paper in his hands and surveyed the room with piercing eyes. *Thorough and calculating*, Jesse decided.

The rhyme on the base read:

You bid me here
Across the land.
The walls that would
Push back the sand,
Built up beneath
My guiding hand.

Something about the lines reminded Jesse of the riddles down in the Rebellion Headquarters. "People from District Two must have liked riddles and rhymes," he muttered to

himself, "even back in ancient times."

"It's not a riddle. It's a poem about a dead person," Owen said, "who I'm not allowed to be disrespectful to."

"Yes, but that doesn't mean the poems aren't mysterious." Jesse glanced back up at Vincent. "Who were these people?"

"Who cares?" Owen replied.

"But why honor a shipbuilder?" Jesse pressed. "Why not a general or an advisor or someone important?"

"Shipbuilders are important," Owen insisted hotly.

Jesse had identified Owen's accent as District One, Jesse's home district, but now he was sure he knew exactly where Owen had lived before the Guard. "You're from the coast of District One, aren't you?" Jesse asked.

Owen nodded. "My father was a merchant," he said. "Is," he quickly added. "At least, I think so. I've been gone for so long...."

There was a lonely sound to that trailed-off sentence. Jesse knew every Youth Guard member could make a statement like that. It was sad, not being able to know for sure what your family was doing while you were gone. *Or, in my case, not knowing if my family is alive.*

"Shipbuilders are important," Jesse said, breaking the silence, "*if* you live in District One, on the coast. But there's no sea near here. No lake, even, unless you count the tar pits or muddy ditches, and I doubt the Lidians did any sailing in *those*."

"Maybe he was important because he was rich," Owen said.

"But why would a shipbuilder come here, of all places, as far away from the sea as possible?" Jesse studied the statue.

"Maybe he wanted to build a miniature fleet for the sovereign's bathtub."

"But he didn't just come," Jesse continued. "He was 'bidden.' Called. Why? And what are the walls that 'push back the sand'?"

"You just won't stop, will you?" Owen muttered. He started to walk toward the staircase, and this time he didn't turn back. "Listen, Jesse, a lot has happened today. You almost died and all that. What say we get some sleep, eh?"

Reluctantly, Jesse turned away. He got the distinct impression that there was something important here. *We'll be back*, he thought. The three figures standing in front of the windows didn't answer, but he was sure they would approve.

Chapter 9

The next morning, with the sun up and streaming through the windows, the old citadel didn't look nearly as frightening as it had the night before. The rugs were bright, with intricate patterns. The faded tapestries on the walls, the ones that weren't torn or burnt, showed cheery scenes of nobles, dancing around blossoming trees. The statues still looked stern, but not nearly as ominous.

It was almost hard for Jesse to believe this was the same city where people vanished, except for the fact that Silas, Parvel and Rae weren't with him anymore.

"I don't understand it," Jesse said, pacing around the room. "How could people wander into the city at night and just… disappear?"

"It's haunted," Owen said, like that was a perfectly reasonable explanation. If anything, a night of sleep had made him even more energetic. "Cursed, by the vanished Lidians and their missing treasure." He grinned.

Jesse knew that grin. They were both from District One,

where stories were prized and the storyteller with the most exciting tales could be the hero of the village.

"Tell me about the missing treasure," Jesse prompted. Owen didn't need any more encouragement. He sat down in the middle of the room on the Lidian crest, and Jesse sat next to him.

"The giants from the mountains in the west attacked Lidia, put it under siege for three months before they finally gave up and broke down the city walls with brute force. Ripped them up with their bare hands."

"No," Jesse corrected. "I saw the damage to the wall around the tower. It looked like the work of a battering ram or catapult."

"They ripped them up with their bare hands," Owen repeated, crossing his arms. "But when they entered the city, there was no one there."

"The people vanished?" Jesse asked. "That's not possible."

"And guess what else?" Owen added, getting excited now. "Their treasure was gone too. Lidia was the richest city ever known to man. They said the sovereign had an entire room lined with gold wallpaper, stamped with designs and a map of the known world. That's why the giants attacked Lidia in the first place; only they didn't find anything in the city but abandoned buildings."

"What happened to the giants?" Jesse asked.

Owen lowered his voice mysteriously. "No one knows. After the attack on Lidia, they were never heard from again. No ambushes on travelers through the mountains. No sign of migration to the northern forests. Most people think the

giants took their families and disappeared into the swamp, never to be seen again."

Never to be seen again. The phrase repeated in Jesse's mind. "How do you know all this?" he asked.

"Barnaby told us. We searched the city twice, looking for any signs of the giants or some kind of message about what happened to them after the attack." Owen shrugged. "Nothing, and no treasure either." Jesse could tell that was what he had been looking for while the others searched for clues to the Giants' Staircase.

Jesse remembered what Parvel said, how nothing more was known of Lidian history after the attack. "And how did Barnaby know all this?"

"I don't know. He lives near here. I guess everyone around the swamps knows."

Jesse stood up, stretching. "Well, I don't believe in curses or ghosts," he said, "so we'll have to find a better explanation for why my squad disappeared."

"Shouldn't we check in the city again?" Owen asked. "They could still be here. I could climb that huge tree in the middle of the town square."

"No," Jesse said immediately, picturing Owen falling to his death. "The branches are dead. Even if you could reach the lowest one, which you can't, it could break off under your weight."

"Could at least try it," Owen muttered, scuffing his shoe on the tile floor.

"Besides, I know they're not here," Jesse said. He couldn't say exactly how he knew. It was a vague feeling of loss—the same he had the day after his parents disappeared. He gestured to the statues around the room. "These are the only residents of the city who can help us now."

For a moment, Owen fell silent, looking back and forth between the three stone figures. "They don't seem to be telling us anything."

"Yes," Jesse said, kneeling down beside Hyram's pedestal. "Yes, they are. I know they are. I just can't figure out what it is."

"Fine," Owen sighed, flopping down on the tile floor and looking at the ceiling. "Tell me when you're done talking to the stone dead men. I'll be right here."

Jesse ran his hands over the lines on Hyram's pedestal. "He was a scribe, a historian," he muttered. "I wonder if he had any followers left at the time of the attack." He raised his voice. "Owen, when you searched the city, did you find a library?"

"Not a single book," Owen replied. He made a face. "Good thing, too, or Nero would have forced us to read every word, looking for some kind of hint about the giants and their staircase."

"Probably destroyed," Jesse muttered, although he couldn't imagine anyone destroying such a great treasure as a library. To him, it would be worth more than the gold-plated room Owen talked about.

Jesse moved around the room to Vincent the shipbuilder. "'The walls that push back the sand.' What walls?" He thought a moment, then snapped his fingers, "the foundations!"

"Right, the foundations," Owen echoed. "Obviously. Great. Now that we've got that figured out, can we find something to eat? I'm hungry."

"Vincent probably laid the foundations of Lidia, pushing back the mud and sand of the swamp," Jesse said, still excited. Then he frowned. "Although why would they would need a shipbuilder to do that instead of a stonemason?"

"Maybe he carved ships out of stone."

"And maybe you don't know what you're talking about," Jesse shot back, starting to lose patience with him.

"I know exactly what I'm talking about," Owen insisted. "I just make it all up."

Jesse rolled his eyes. He walked slowly over to the last statue, Jardos the sovereign. "Why call the city 'the noble hill'?"

"Because it's on a hill," Owen practically yelled. "How more obvious can it be?"

"But Jardos ruled the city, not the hill," Jesse said. "Maybe it means something."

"Maybe it means you're crazy."

That was it. "Time to get something to eat," Jesse said, walking toward the door. He couldn't tolerate Owen's complaints any longer.

Owen did a flip to spring to his feet. "About time," he moaned, clutching his stomach.

Jesse turned around quickly, looking behind them. Nothing was moving. He could almost feel Jardos' piercing stone eyes watching him walk out of the tower.

"I know a great orchard near the market street," Owen said, pulling on Jesse's arm. "I fell asleep there the last time we were in the city."

"Well, you were clearly very useful to your squad."

"I'm a growing boy," Owen protested. "I need my rest."

"Breakfast, then we search the city," Jesse said. He checked the streets before letting Owen dart out. No one was there.

"Again?" Owen demanded. "I told you, we checked *everything*!"

"You were looking for a staircase, not..." Jesse's voice trailed off. What *would* they look for? "Not three missing people."

"They vanished," Owen said ominously. "The Swamp of the Vanished never gives anyone back."

"Then we'll have to take them back," Jesse said, fixing his face in determination.

"Why can't we just *leave*?" Owen whined. "I want to go home."

"So do I," Jesse said, "but if you go home, and *especially* if I go home, the king and his Riders will kill us."

Owen stared at Jesse, wrinkling his freckled nose. "You're not joking after all, are you? You really mean it."

Jesse nodded. "They know what we look like and where we live. In fact, there's a one-hundred-sceptre reward on my head."

Owen gave a long whistle. "I'd turn you in for that much."

"Thanks. That's very comforting."

But at least now Owen wasn't acting like this was all a grand adventure. A trace of seriousness had entered his blue eyes. "That long story you were telling me about?" he said. "Now's as good a time as any to hear it, eh?"

So, as they walked through the city to the orchard, Jesse told him, starting from the very beginning. It took a long time, because Owen interrupted after what seemed like every sentence.

"And here we were wandering around in a giant tar pit for a month," he grumbled when Jesse had finished, taking a big bite out of the fruit he held. "You got to have all the fun."

"I would be happy to have a little less 'fun' if it means I'm not running for my life every day," Jesse shot back. He had a neat pile of fruit stems next to him, but a look at the number of stems scattered around Owen's feet told him that he had eaten twice as many. "You're going to get sick, you know," he said, even though he knew he sounded like Silas.

Owen was looking on the ground for something. "Any brilliant ideas to find those friends of yours? Because you're not leaving without them, and I'm not going into the swamp on my own."

Jesse couldn't resist the urge to tease him. "What, are you afraid?"

"No," Owen said, picking up a fruit. He squeezed it slightly, and Jesse could tell it was rotten. "I just don't like swamps." He changed the subject abruptly. "Bet I can't hit that pot?"

"What pot?" Jesse asked, looking around.

"The one in the windowsill. Three stories up, to the right."

Jesse looked where Owen was pointing. He could hardly see the pot. "I'll take that bet."

With a mischievous little grin, Owen reached back and threw the rotten fruit so hard that Jesse barely saw it before it sent the pot clattering faintly inside the building.

"You lost," Owen informed him, the mischievous grin creeping up again.

Jesse stood and began to pace. "Great. Wonderful. Good aim. Now, if you want to leave this city alive, help me think of what to do." He paused. "No. Forget I said that. Let *me* think of what to do."

Something in Owen seemed to sag, but then he shrugged. "Fine."

If only one of the others were here with me, Jesse thought. *They were always so good at making decisions. Coming up with a plan. I don't even know where to start.*

And what if they're not even alive?

Jesse shook his head, dismissing the thought. Instead, he focused on Owen's story. "How did a city of four hundred people escape during a siege?"

"You know, for claiming you're not crazy, you sure talk to yourself a lot."

It was Owen, of course. He had moved on from target practice to balancing on the orchard wall, teetering from side to side as he hopped on one foot.

"Get down from there," Jesse said half-heartedly. Somehow, he didn't think Owen would fall. *Or if he did, he'd land on his feet.*

"Don't worry, I won't fall," Owen said. "Anyway, it's not very high. Once, I…."

Jesse didn't hear the rest of what he said. Instead, he focused on the history of Lidia, letting Owen chatter away in the background.

"Tunnels," Jesse said suddenly.

"Newts," Owen said. "Fenceposts. Rutabagas. Is this a game? Blurt out random words without explaining why?"

"No. Listen. Unless they knew how to fly, the Lidians had to use tunnels to get out of the city when the giants put it under siege," Jesse explained.

Owen laughed. "I don't think that would work. You fell into the tar pit. You know what the ground here is like. They'd practically have to swim to get out of there."

"Then who better than a shipbuilder, trained in keeping out water, to construct the tunnels?" Jesse said triumphantly. "What if the walls that pushed back the sand were real walls… walls with space in between?"

"Then there would be tunnels underneath the city. Why should I care?"

Jesse knew why he cared. If the Lidians had disappeared through the tunnels, there was a good chance that Parvel, Silas and Rae had too.

"That might be where the Lidians hid their treasure," Jesse said, watching Owen carefully.

"I'll search this side of the city. You can go east," Owen said cheerfully, jumping down from the wall.

"No," Jesse said firmly. "We stay together. Understood?"

"Fine," Owen said, sighing loudly, "if I have to."

"I should be the one that's complaining. I have to listen to you and keep you from killing yourself."

"But you're covered in dried tar," Owen pointed out, "and you smell bad."

Jesse just gritted his teeth. *By the end of today, the ruins of Lidia might just have a new ghost.*

Chapter 10

Several hours later, Jesse and Owen had found only an abandoned tinker's cart, a melon patch and a huge, hairy spider that Owen let crawl over his arm before Jesse made him kill it.

Finally, they stopped for a break under the dead tree at the center of the city. Jesse sat down underneath its towering branches, wishing the answer would just fall from the sky.

Why can't we find them? He sighed loudly. *Maybe we should wait here until nightfall, then shout and wave our arms around so we'll get taken too.*

"I'm thirsty," Owen moaned, plopping down beside him. It was the latest in a long string of complaints, which also included hunger, boredom, soreness and an allergy to old, crumbling buildings.

"We can go down the hill and drink some swamp water," Jesse suggested wearily, closing his eyes.

"No," Owen said, shaking his head. "There's a well in the courtyard. We refilled our canteens there before." He sprang up and Jesse limped after him, wondering at how Owen never seemed to run out of energy, no matter how much he complained about being tired.

Once inside the walls, Jesse realized he had been in the courtyard before. It was the one with the phases-of-the-moon design in the center.

Owen was already at the well in the corner, yanking on a rope like he was a sailor hauling up a load of cargo.

"Don't fall in," Jesse warned him. That was all he needed to deal with: fishing an eleven-year-old out of a well.

Jesse took his time joining him. *Strange*. The rope appeared to be in better shape than the rest of the city. It was still taut and strong, without any sign of wear.

Owen dropped the bucket twice before he managed to haul it up, half full, but Jesse wasn't about to criticize.

Jesse had to admit he was thirsty. Except for the fruit they had eaten for breakfast, he hadn't had anything to drink since the day before. He took the bucket after Owen and drank from it.

His stomach growled, reminding him how much walking they had done in one morning. "I suppose it's more fruit for our afternoon meal."

But Owen was already running around the courtyard, exploring. "I guess I'll bring it to you," Jesse called, rolling his eyes.

"Thanks!" Owen said, scrambling over a fallen pillar.

"Just don't leave the courtyard," Jesse said, using his sternest tone. He surveyed the courtyard, trying to remember how to get to the vineyard.

There. Down the steps.

Sure enough, the vineyard with the yellow fruit lay at the bottom of the steps. The dark vines, tangled around the stone walls, were exactly the same as Jesse remembered them. But there was something wrong.

Jesse returned empty-handed. "Where's the food?" Owen demanded. Now he was up in a tree by the courtyard wall.

"There wasn't any fruit," Jesse said, shaking his head. "No ripe fruit, anyway."

"So this patch is a little slow," Owen said, shrugging. "Let's go back to the orchard where we got breakfast. Or, I guess there's that melon patch a few houses over."

"No, you don't understand," Jesse said. "I was just here yesterday, and those vines were sagging with ripe fruit."

"You sure you have the right place? I mean, there's not much that's special about a bunch of vines."

"Maybe..." Jesse said, trying to think back. But the scene from the day before played out in his mind exactly the same way every time: he ate a fruit from the vineyard, then came up the steps and saw Parvel in the courtyard with the phases of the moon.

"Jesse," Owen said, and his tone of voice made Jesse snap his head up instantly. "There are people coming."

"Get down from there," Jesse hissed, scanning the courtyard for a hiding place. The well was too short, the tree not wide enough. Up the porch steps and inside the building? Not enough time.

Owen didn't bother to climb down using the branches. He just dropped from the tree, landing hard, but on his feet. Jesse hoped whoever was in the city hadn't heard the sound.

They both ran for the same place: the pile of crumbled pillars across the courtyard near the building. Owen scrambled over the top of one while Jesse went around. He crouched down and tried to make himself as small as possible.

He could hear voices approaching now as well as footsteps. Two people, both men.

"...wouldn't hope to find them here, in these ruins," one was saying. Jesse didn't recognize the voice, and he didn't dare bring his face up over the pillar. "Even if they chanced to be here, there is too much ground to cover. I say we return to the camp with Lillen."

"I don't like this city," another voice said.

This one Jesse recognized, and the sound made him sink even farther down behind the crumbled stone. Captain Demetri. Somehow, he had traveled across the country and found them again.

And this time, Captain Demetri isn't alone.

"Most prefer to avoid the ruins," the other man said. "It has become more legend than reality. Haunted by Lidians, some say, the home of the Westlund giants, according to others, and a wandering place for the spirits of vanished Amarian travelers, others insist."

Oddly, the second man's voice had a kind of lilting quality to it, like an actor in a theatre troupe. Somehow, it made Jesse want to lean in and listen.

"Do you fear the city, Captain?" he asked.

Captain Demetri made a derisive sound. "I do not hold to those weak superstitions. I don't like this city because there are too many places to hide."

He paused, and Jesse's heart beat faster. He could almost feel Captain Demetri's eyes on the pillars.

"At least we know why we haven't received reports from the Rider assigned to the swamp," the other man said. "The state of the camp was peculiar, to say the least. Wouldn't you agree, Captain?"

"No," Captain Demetri said firmly. "He was ambushed, probably by the very squad he sought to kill."

"And what of the boy—Barnaby, wasn't it? The squad captain and the girl said he entered the ruins and never came out."

"Nero and Talia?" Owen mouthed, a question written in his eyes.

Jesse nodded. It had to be.

"There must be a logical explanation," Captain Demetri said. "I refuse to believe otherwise."

Jesse almost admired his confidence. He was nearly beginning to waver in that belief. The strange history of the city, the eeriness of the ruins at night, the way everyone who entered mysteriously disappeared…it didn't seem natural.

"Perhaps," the second man said. "Should I give Lillen the order to kill the two we found?"

Owen whimpered, but Jesse kept his eyes fixed straight ahead and his hand firmly on Owen's shoulder to keep him from doing anything foolish.

"No," Captain Demetri said. "Keep them alive. The Four are looking for the other squad. If we hold our two captives prisoner, they will come to us."

"You really believe that?" the second man asked, a note of

skepticism in his voice. "They would risk their lives to save two strangers? It doesn't seem likely."

"You haven't met these four, Ward," Captain Demetri said bitterly. "Nothing they do is 'likely'."

Jesse felt a surge of pride. He was one of the four that Captain Demetri spoke of, even though he did not belong to the Youth Guard. *And I am a key reason we're still alive*, he thought, remembering the times he saved his squad members' lives.

"If they're alive, they will come," Captain Demetri said. His voice began to fade as he walked away from them. "If they're not alive...well, then our work is done."

"No, Captain," Ward said, giving a faint chuckle. "We are Riders. Our work is never done. There are always others."

In that moment, Jesse knew that these men would kill them without the slightest twinge of guilt. They would destroy the Youth Guard by eliminating its members, one by one. This was no game.

Owen started to move forward, but Jesse held him down. He couldn't take the chance that Captain Demetri and Ward were still there, waiting and watching for them.

"What do we do?" Owen whispered. He was fiddling nervously with something, and Jesse knew the overheard conversation had made him realize the seriousness of what was happening.

Jesse shifted to take the pressure off of his throbbing knees. The stone of the courtyard was not a comfortable surface to crouch on. "I don't know," he said, feeling helpless. Now, they didn't dare continue their search of the city. There was no telling when Captain Demetri and Ward would leave, and Jesse, for one, did not want to take any chances.

Owen dropped the object he was holding, and it clattered to the ground. "Sorry," Owen said, wincing and glancing over his shoulder.

Jesse looked at the object for the first time. It was the golden dial, the one Silas had found in the swamp outside of the city. "Where did you get that?"

He clutched it protectively, as if afraid that Jesse would try to take it from him. "Why do you want to know?"

"Because the last person to hold that was Parvel," Jesse said.

"But it's mine now," Owen insisted. "I found it."

"Owen, I'm not trying to steal your new toy," Jesse said, frustration creeping in. "Now, think carefully. Was the dial tipped over on its side like someone had dropped it, or was it standing up?"

Owen paused, turning the dial around in his hands. "Standing up."

If I were Parvel and someone was taking me away, what would I do?

The answer was obvious. *Leave a sign.*

"Owen, this is very important," Jesse said. "Where was the dial, and where was its tip pointing?"

"It was by the steps," Owen said, standing and nodding at the steps to the porch of the building facing the courtyard. "Pointing inside."

"Then that's where we're going."

As Jesse climbed the steps, he pictured Parvel pausing to

set down the dial, perhaps faking a stumble. At night, in the dark, who would notice?

"They have to be here," he said, more confidently than he felt, "somewhere."

And they have to be alive.

The building was more ornate than the tower they had spent the night in. Its high ceilings were held up by scrolled pillars, and the furniture, chopped into firewood-sized pieces, showed detailed carvings that even Kayne would have admired.

"This place was totally destroyed," Owen said, almost in a tone of admiration.

He was right. Almost nothing but the walls and floors were left intact. Windowsills had deep gouges in them. Torch holders lay fallen on the ground. Even the thick carpets had been torn in places, and lay half-rolled up in the center of the room.

"This must have been the sovereign's palace," Jesse said. "The Westlunders probably thought the treasure would be here and ransacked the building looking for it."

"So it's probably not here, eh?" Owen asked glumly.

"We're not looking for treasure anyway," Jesse reminded him. "Search the rooms, carefully. Don't bother with the upstairs chambers. We're looking for an entrance to an underground tunnel. Understand?"

When there was no answer, Jesse turned to see Owen glaring while stroking an imaginary beard, imitating the stern posture of a man in a painting on the wall. "What?" he demanded, in response to Jesse's look.

"Get to work," Jesse said, "unless you want to spend another night in Lidia."

With a loud sigh, Owen darted over to the long hallway. Jesse could hear his voice echoing from one of the rooms. "There's a suit of armor in here! It's huge, and I think it has real blood on it!"

Jesse hobbled over to an adjoining room. He suddenly knew why the Patrol let an eleven-year-old join the Youth Guard. Owen had spent a month living in the swamps with very little food, and he was still as full of energy as if he had just been released from the village school for the harvest season.

The room next to the main entrance seemed to be a small dining hall. The table had been hacked to pieces. Jesse found one of its legs and let out a low whistle. It came up to his neck. *The regent must have wanted large furniture,* he thought. *Perhaps to look more impressive.*

Nothing looked impressive any more. The cabinet nearby was empty of any contents, doors hanging open on bent hinges. A deck of cards, printed with emblems representing the four seasons, were scattered around the room.

Jesse walked across a sleek black bearskin rug that seemed to growl at the mess in front of him. He didn't see anything he recognized, nothing from Parvel's pack that he might have left behind.

He searched the kitchen, connected to the dining hall by a small servant's door, and then the main dining hall and a ballroom. Nothing.

"Owen?" Jesse called into the hallway. He hadn't heard anything being dropped in a while.

Owen popped out from the doorway across the hall. "Last room. This place *feels* more haunted. We should sleep here tonight."

"That's a terrible reason to want to sleep here."

"No, it's not!"

"But you didn't find anything?" Jesse asked, just to make sure.

"Just a plant that eats insects," Owen said. "That's what the carving on the pot said, anyway." He looked down the hallway. "Have you seen any flies?"

Doubt started to creep into Jesse's mind. What if Parvel had dropped the dial on accident? Or what if there was more than one broken dial in the ruins?

No. Rae, at least, would tell him to keep trying—to never give up, no matter how bad things looked.

"You're talking to yourself again," Owen said, and Jesse realized he had been muttering his thoughts out loud.

"There has to be something here," Jesse said. "Something strange or out of place."

"*Everything's* out of place," Owen pointed out.

He was right. It would be easier to track Parvel if the house were neat and in perfect order. Then there would be disturbances, ways to see where someone had passed by. Here, though, with everything in complete disorder....

Wait. That was it.

"Not everything is out of place," Jesse said, going back to the smaller dining hall.

"What's that supposed to mean?" Owen grumbled, following him.

"Look at this room," Jesse said, standing in the doorway. "What's wrong with it? What's different than every other room we've been in?"

Owen elbowed his way past and looked in. "Hmm," he said thoughtfully. "Furniture chopped up, stuff thrown around, no treasure anywhere...it looks exactly the same as every other room."

"The rug," Jesse offered helpfully. "What's wrong with it?"

"It's dead." Owen got on his knees and put his ear to the bear's snout. "He doesn't know where your friends are either," he reported.

"Doesn't anything about it seem odd?" Jesse pressed.

"Just tell me already," Owen said. "You and Nero are both the same. Always trying to get me to play your little logic games. I joined the Youth Guard to get *away* from school."

Jesse gave up. "There are cards scattered all over the room, but not on the rug. And the other rugs and carpets in the building are torn and thrown to the side. This one is laying neatly on the floor...almost like it's hiding something."

That was all Owen needed. He pulled up on the bear's paw. The rug lifted, and with it, a heavy wooden door in the floorboards.

For a moment, Jesse just stared. They had found the entrance to the Lidian tunnels!

Owen pushed the door open all the way, letting it slam backward to the floor. "Looks safe to me," he said. "Let's go!"

"We are *not* going down there without a light," Jesse said firmly, pushing the door back down. He felt strange, being the responsible one. He usually left that job to Silas and Parvel.

Jesse lit a small oil lamp from the kitchen—the glow was faint, but exactly what they needed. A torch would create too much light. *We don't want to attract attention to ourselves. Who knows what we'll find down those steps?*

"I'll take that," Owen said, snatching the lamp, almost blowing out the flame in the process. "I want to go first."

He ran back to the dining hall and sat on the edge of the hole created by the trapdoor, swinging his legs into the dark. "I'm going to jump."

"There's a ladder," Jesse said, pointing to its dim outline against the wall.

"Oh," Owen said. He sounded almost disappointed. Still, he grabbed onto the ladder and started to climb down, holding the rungs with one hand and the lamp with the other.

"Are you afraid of anything?" Jesse asked.

Owen seemed to think about that. "Let's see…tests in school." He went deeper into the shaft. "My aunt's cooking." A pause, and Jesse was afraid he had disappeared until he added, "And grubs. Hate those things."

Jesse climbed down after him, shutting the door behind them and testing for the bottom with his staff as he went. There was a strange rancid smell in the air. Somehow, he was sure he had smelled it before.

When he reached the bottom, he took a few steps to the left, and something crunched under his feet. Owen jerked around, and the light fell on the ground for a few seconds.

Crushed glass. Why is there glass underground?

"It's just an old wine cellar," Owen said, shining the lamp

on the walls, where wooden racks hung, some splintered, some intact.

That would explain the glass...and the smell. It was exactly the same as the smell of Roddy's Haunt, the abandoned tavern they had found in the capital of District Two.

"There must be something..." Jesse began. He stopped, looking at the ground again. "Owen, shine the light on the floor, please." He did, and Jesse pointed. "See? Right underneath the ladder, the glass has been ground into powder. Because—"

"A lot of people have walked on it," Owen finished, following the trail of pulverized glass, which led to the back corner of the wine cellar.

"There's a staircase!" Owen crowed. Only a few steps were visible before they turned into darkness.

Of course. The tunnels, if they existed, would have to be much farther down than one level underneath the city streets.

"Should we take it?" Jesse asked, knowing right away what Owen's answer would be.

He was already climbing down the stairs, and Jesse joined him. *Down to find Parvel, Silas and Rae.* At least, Jesse hoped so. He had to acknowledge what they were doing: creeping, weaponless, to a passage beneath a haunted city. *We could easily become two of the vanished.*

No. Not me. I've challenged death before and come out alive, Jesse reminded himself. But, although his words were confident, he had to force himself to take the first few steps below the lost city of Lidia.

Chapter 11

Of all the things Jesse expected to find in the underground tunnels, an ankle-deep layer of water was not one of them.

"Tunnels below the city?" Owen asked skeptically, jerking the lamp around to inspect the room at the bottom of the steps. The sudden movements were starting to make Jesse dizzy. "More like a sewer."

"No, it's clean water," Jesse said, studying it in the dim light of the oil lamp. "I think."

Already his boots were soaked, except for the two small patches that Rae had sewn. She did good work. Thinking about Rae gave Jesse enough courage to keep going into the darkness.

"I would fire that shipbuilder," Owen grumbled. "I could do better work than this."

The walls of the tunnel were stone, held together with some kind of sticky black pitch. Jesse wondered how long it took the Lidians to build the tunnels. They seemed to go on for a long way. If the Lidians had indeed used them to escape the siege, they would have to at least go past the walls of the city.

"Hey, look," Owen said, stopping after only a few watery steps. He pointed up. There, wrapping around the top of the stone like a border, was the familiar glowing stone that Jesse had come to associate with District Two.

Jesse took a step forward and craned his neck. Instead of being cramped, like the mines in the Suspicion Mountains, the ceilings of these tunnels were high and perfectly formed, supported here and there by graceful pillars. *Nothing but the best for the Lidians.* He squinted. *And is that—?*

"Well, that's a nice decoration," Owen said, jerking the lamp away suddenly and heading farther down the tunnel.

"Wait," Jesse whispered, motioning him back. "I think I see something written on the border."

Owen sighed and trudged back. "I was hoping you wouldn't notice. Shouldn't we get going in case the giants come?"

"They're probably outside of the city, where these tunnels lead," Jesse reasoned. He thought of the stories that told of giants crushing a farmer's cart with one careless step. "They'd have to crawl to get through these tunnels, so they couldn't stay here for long. But we'll keep our voices low, just in case," he added. No need to take unnecessary risks.

He turned his attention back to the border. Since the words were high on the wall, it was difficult to read them, but the letters themselves were crisp and clear even after hundreds of years underground.

Not all who vanish are truly lost.
Not all that is missing is gone.
Some melt away like the morning frost.
Some will return come the dawn.

Those who dare to pay the cost
Will shout this from the sky:
Not all who vanish are truly lost,
The Noble Hill will never die!

"That's what they thought," Owen muttered. "Sure looks dead to me."

"No civilization lasts forever," Jesse said, shrugging. "Someday, even our capital, Terenid, and other Amarian cities will look like Lidia."

"Then who lived here before us?" Owen asked. "Before Amarias?"

Jesse thought about it. He had learned some history in school, but none of it ever went back past the reign of Marias, the first king, who named his kingdom after himself. "I don't know," he admitted.

He looked again at the poem. He had heard one of the lines before, and recently: 'Not all that is missing is gone.' Then he remembered. *Margo*. She had quoted it as a proverb of the Kin. *I wonder where she heard it?*

As usual, that subject no longer held Owen's attention. He had scrambled over to the opposite wall. "Look, more writing," he said, pointing just over his head.

There, words and letters had been gouged out, and Jesse was only able to make out part of the inscription. The farther down the inscription, the more letters were missing.

THRE G V THE R ALL
FOR LI IA'S CAL
S N OF AMA AS
LIDI SON
SON OF WES L D
J IN AS O
TH R SA IF CE
O GR ES PR
EALS T E KEY.
TO L A' WE L
ND T Y

"Strange," Jesse said. "These words were painted, not carved—as if they were added later…and in a hurry." He touched a letter and a piece of paint flaked away. "Time has not been kind to this inscription. Look how much is missing."

"That would explain the bad spelling," Owen said. "I was having a hard time reading it."

Jesse was already trying to fill in the missing words. "I can see 'Lidia' a few times," he muttered. "That must be 'Amarias.' The first line probably has the word 'their'…."

"I don't believe this," Owen said, grabbing Jesse's arms. "Remember, we went down a trapdoor into a secret tunnel so we could rescue your friends—not to stare at a musty old poem *again*."

"But it might be important," Jesse protested.

"It's a poem. I don't care what it's about. It's boring." Owen dragged Jesse into the tunnel. He marched straight down it, while Jesse stopped to look in the arched rooms that led off the main tunnel on either side.

Strange. There was a faint light coming from one of the side rooms. *More glowing stone?* Jesse slogged through the water and peered in.

"Forget poetry. I'd rather find a ghost guarding a room full of treasure, or an old bridge across a pit of snakes—"

"Or a Lidian prison," Jesse suggested.

"With bones for the bars," Owen added.

"No," Jesse said, grabbing Owen's arm and pulling him back to the side room. "I was being serious."

There were four prisoners sitting on benches, their arms and ankles chained to the wall. The flickering torches showed that their bodies were limp and slumped in different positions. For one terrible moment, Jesse was afraid they were dead.

Then he saw their chests moving, and he started to breathe again himself. "Asleep," he said, noticing the same fearful expression on Owen's face.

"Oh," Owen said, stepping into the room. The water was lower here, and they managed to cross over to the prisoners without waking them.

Now Jesse could see the details of the prisoner's faces. To his relief, Parvel, Rae and Silas were all among them. The last was a boy Jesse immediately recognized from the picture in the Forbidden Book, down to the feathers tucked behind his ear.

"Barnaby," Owen whispered, grinning. "I knew he was still alive." He turned to Jesse. "Should we wake them?"

Something screeched in Jesse's ear. He jumped back instinctively, looking all around. There, peering out from behind Barnaby's thick, curly hair, was a small black bird.

"Hello, Zora," Owen said, reaching out to touch the bird. She pecked at his hand, and he jerked it back. "Nice to see you too."

"I am going to kill that bird," Rae muttered, slowly stretching her arms as far as they could go in the chains. Then she opened her eyes. "Jesse?"

"Jesse!" Parvel exclaimed, his sleepy eyes widening in surprise. "Thank God you're alive."

Silas, as usual, was the last to wake, and did not look happy. "But he's here, and that's something you should probably *not* be thanking your God for."

Never had Silas' dry, sensible comments sounded so good.

"We wondered when you were going to show up," Rae grumbled. "Any hope of breaking us out of here?"

"I can rip these chains right off the wall," Owen offered, jumping up on the bench and yanking at the metal plate that bolted the chains to the stone. In the process, he managed to jerk Rae's arms backward.

"Who is he?" she asked Jesse, not amused by Owen's antics.

"One of the squad members we've been looking for," Jesse said. "I see you've met another one." He nodded at Barnaby. "I'm Jesse."

"Barnaby," he said, "but you already know that. You met my family."

There was a trace of disgust in his voice, and Jesse wondered how much of their conversation Parvel had told him.

"Unless you want to join us in this prison, I suggest you leave," Parvel said. "They check on us every now and then. The intervals vary—these Westlunders do not seem to be the organized, methodical types."

"Wait, the Westlunders?" Jesse asked, confused. "They're the ones who brought you here?" Parvel nodded. "How did they get down here? They're giants…right?"

"In a way," Silas said. "They're taller than any of us, but not by much. We couldn't understand them, but they didn't seem very happy that we had been wandering around the city."

Owen jumped down from the bench, giving up his plan of wrenching the chains off the wall. "So, where are the keys?" he asked, looking around.

"They keep them in a jar in the middle of the room with a sign that says, 'Here, prisoners, escape!'" Barnaby put in.

"Now I remember why I was glad you disappeared," Owen said, making a face at him. Zora stuck her head out and cawed angrily. Owen quickly jerked back. "You too, Zora."

"No sign of the Rider?" Jesse asked. "The one whose camp we found?"

"He died fighting," Silas said grimly. "Used a knife to kill two of them before they brought him down. One of the giants speaks Amarian and told us this as they took us down, as a warning not to try to get away."

Jesse was about to ask where the giants on guard duty slept when he noticed Silas was staring fixedly at the archway.

"Shh!" Jesse commanded Owen. He knew that expression. Silas heard something. "They're coming," Silas said, as calmly and confidently as if he were talking about the weather.

Jesse trusted him, even though he didn't hear anything at all. With things like this, Silas was never wrong. A quick glance around the room told him that there was no other way out. *And there's no place to hide, unless there's another trap door somewhere.*

"Come on," Jesse hissed, bolting for the doorway. "Maybe we can outrun them."

The good thing about giant footsteps, especially in a flooded tunnel, is that you can hear them from a long way off, a detached part of Jesse's brain realized as he ran.

And, as soon as they stop, they'll be able to hear us.

Jesse sloshed through the watery halls as quickly as he could, but Owen was already out of sight. *We can't outrun them—at least, I can't.*

Suddenly, Jesse felt himself being jerked backward into an arched opening in the wall. The only thing that kept him from crying out was the fact that the hand wasn't a giant's. In fact, it was rather small.

He whirled around to face Owen, who was staring into the darkness of the main passageway. He had either blown out the oil lamp or dropped it in the watery tunnels. Only the dim light of the glowing stone allowed him to see at all. "We hide here and hope they don't find us," he explained.

It took a few seconds for Jesse's eyes to adjust, before he looked around. Owen had dragged them into a short tunnel.

His heart started pounding harder. The tunnel was filled

with figures wrapped in cloth, a chalky gray against the black stone. The bodies—he assumed they were bodies, for none of them moved—were lying in shallow outcroppings in the wall. A strip of glowing stone outlined each outcropping.

"Owen," Jesse began, feeling his throat tighten up.

"Dead end," Owen said, peering out the jagged entrance. The footsteps and voices were still coming. "And we're going to be the dead ones."

"I think someone already stole that position from us," Jesse managed.

"What are you…?" Owen's voice trailed off as he turned around. "Oh."

That was all. Jesse expected him to get excited, to start talking about how skeletons were much more interesting than historical ruins. But he just stood there, looking at the remains of previous visitors to the tunnels.

That was fine with Jesse. After all, these bodies had once been living, breathing people just like them. Maybe they had met some kind of terrible death in these very tunnels. There was no way to know for sure.

He froze. The voices were right outside the tunnel now. From their tone, it sounded like they were angry about something.

But instead of reaching in a huge fist and pulling Jesse and Owen out of the tomb, the voices and footsteps began to fade, along with the orange torchlight.

Jesse didn't dare look out the opening at the giants. He didn't even move until well after the tunnel became silent again. "Should we go back to the prison?" he asked Owen.

But Owen was already getting a closer look at the bones. Apparently any momentary reverence he felt in the presence of the dead was gone. "I guess these folks won't betray us to the giants, eh?"

Jesse backed up, giving one last look to the main tunnel before he joined Owen to examine the bodies. They were of normal height—not Westlunders then. Each compartment held one body. Jesse did a quick count, pacing along the length of the hallway. There were fifteen compartments lining the shallow tunnel. Eleven were occupied.

One body had a brass compass at his side. Another was draped in a fancy red coat with a silk handkerchief poking out of the pocket. One had even been left with a fine, sturdy leather bag, the design of a falcon burned into it.

It must be some strange Westlund tradition of burying the dead. Briefly, Jesse wondered which one was the Guard Rider who had camped in the ruins, but he decided not to try to find out.

"It's a burial crypt," Jesse said. "Instead of putting them in the ground, they laid them out here, with their possessions."

"Why didn't any of these dead people possess weapons?" Owen demanded, rummaging through the bones in one compartment. He glanced up at Jesse. "And *don't* tell me I'm being disrespectful to the dead. We can use all the help we can get down here."

I guess he's right. Still, stealing from a dead body seemed like a terrible thing.

"Just our luck," Owen muttered, disgusted. "This girl had a scabbard, but no sword."

"Girl?" Jesse asked, joining Owen at one of the compartments.

There lay a small skeleton draped in a torn dress of deep, rich blue with an empty scabbard at her side. An intricate silver necklace was around her neck, molded into the shape of a butterfly. It reminded Jesse of the token he carried for Barnaby. *I forgot to give it to him.*

"She wasn't much taller than me," Owen said, a little sadly.

Jesse nodded. "I guess we'll never know what she was doing in the swamps."

"She die here," a loud voice said.

Startled, Jesse jerked around, but saw no one. *Are the bones talking?* Immediately, Jesse knew the thought was ridiculous.

"She one of the Vanished," the voice continued. Now Jesse could tell the voice came from beyond the entryway. "Before I Watcher, when more die."

"Shh!" Owen ordered the voice from the darkness. "You'll bring them down here."

A pause. "Yes. I have to bring them." The voice switched to the strange, guttural language of the giants.

Jesse glanced around. There was nowhere to go. Within seconds, they heard heavy steps and loud voices approach from the other direction.

"We're trapped," Owen hissed. He climbed into one of the compartments.

"Owen, you can't hide behind a body," Jesse said, pulling him back. He had decided to face the intruders. *After all, they didn't kill Silas, Rae, Parvel or Barnaby. Maybe they won't kill us either.*

But what about the girl with the silver necklace and these ten others? another part of him pointed out.

"They come to get you," the voice explained.

Sure enough, the splashing footsteps became louder, and two giants stepped into the crypt. They didn't look like Jesse had pictured them. They didn't have to crawl into the room, although the first stooped slightly, his head nearly grazing the rock ceiling. Jesse's head only reached the giants' waists, and the effect was much like being a young child in the presence of large, strong adults.

The giants discussed something with each other for a minute, gesturing to Jesse and Owen. Neither of the voices matched the first one they had heard from the crypt.

One put a large hand on Jesse's shoulders, leaning down to look at him, then stopped, staring. He pointed to Jesse's neck with a thick finger.

It was the token, Barnaby's token, that lay against Jesse's torn, stained shirt. One of the giants snatched at it, breaking the cord in one swift motion. He held it up to his eye. Jesse knew that if the token seemed small to him, it was tiny to the giant.

"Bird," he said, stroking its back with one finger. Then he looked down at Jesse, squinting, and spoke again.

He and the other giant spoke with each other hurriedly. Jesse heard one word repeated often: *castor*. He hoped that didn't mean "torture" or "death" in the giants' language.

One of the giants leaned down to face Jesse, a strange look on his face. It wasn't the wide, dull grin that Jesse had always pictured on a giant. It was crafty and greedy, and very intelligent. He gave the token back to Jesse.

"What are you going to do with us?" Jesse demanded, more for Owen than anything else.

He was surprised when the voice from the passageway spoke again, carefully pronouncing each word. "You are third son. Many years, we wait for you."

Chapter 12

The owner of the mysterious voice was another giant, one nearly a head shorter than the other two. He had reddish-brown hair and strong features that reminded Jesse of someone he had seen before. A peacock feather stuck out of his cloth cap. *It's the only feather that would be large enough for a hat like that,* Jesse realized.

"You two come with me," he said, "to my home."

He turned to the other giants and translated what he had said into the Westlund language. At first, they didn't seem to agree, growling something at the translator that Jesse assumed was an insult. They pointed down the hallway, and Jesse knew they wanted to take them to the prison with the others.

To be honest, Jesse would have almost preferred that. He had been without his squad members for too long. They could come up with a plan to escape. *But, for some reason, I'm no longer an average prisoner.*

After a heated argument with the other two giants, the translator smiled triumphantly. "Come," he said. "Not stay in prison with others. Stay with me." He began to walk in the opposite direction, away from the prison, gesturing for them to follow him.

For a moment, Jesse considered running back to the wine cellar staircase. *We'd never make it. Now that we've been found, we can't run.*

"The third son?" Jesse said to Owen as they slogged through the water after the translator. "What does that mean?"

"Maybe you're related to the Westlunders somehow," Owen said. "Barnaby told us that in the old days, some Westlunders left their tribe in the mountains and married average people."

Jesse just stared at him. "Owen, look at me. Do I look like I have even one drop of giant blood in my body?"

Owen studied him critically, then nodded. "I guess you're right."

The translator stopped before one of the archways set in the wall. "My home," he said, letting them go in before him. There was no door, not even a curtain. *Apparently, the Westlunders don't care much for privacy.*

Inside, the translator's home looked much like any house belonging to an Amarian, except a measurement or two larger. There was a brick oven in the corner with a chimney to release smoke above the ground. *That explains the smoke I saw coming from the grate in the city streets*, Jesse thought.

Interestingly, the translator had a writing desk in the corner of the room, next to a large bookshelf. Jesse walked over to it, glancing at the titles. All were written in a strange, thick lettering that mimicked the sound of the giant's language.

A table, a bench and one large stuffed chair made up the rest of the furnishings. There was a door leading into another room, where Jesse assumed the translator slept.

"Castor, son of Mardon," the translator said, pointing to himself. "Welcome to Below-Lidia."

"Clever name," Jesse said dryly.

"Hello, Clever," Castor said seriously, reaching out to shake Jesse's hand.

"No," Jesse said quickly, realizing his mistake. "That's not my name. I was talking about the name of the...." He shook his head. "Never mind. I'm Jesse."

"Owen," Owen said.

"Who taught you how to speak Amarian?" Jesse said, making sure to talk slowly.

"Man named Gideon," Castor said.

"One of our skeleton friends in the crypt?" Owen asked. "Did you kill him?"

Every time one of them spoke, Castor would stare down at them with serious brown eyes, listening with every fiber of his being. He must have understood the word "kill," because as soon as Owen said it, he shook his head furiously, knocking it into the chandelier.

"No," he said, rubbing his head. "He alive. In Westlund."

Westlund. Hadn't the Westlund settlements in the mountains been abandoned? Jesse exchanged glances with Owen, who shrugged.

"Where is Westlund?" Jesse asked.

Castor shrugged and pointed up and toward the far wall.

"East," Owen supplied immediately.

"How can you possibly know that?" Jesse demanded. He wasn't even sure which direction was up anymore.

"I'm sure," was all Owen said.

Castor pointed toward the wall again. "East?" he asked.

Jesse nodded. "South. West. North," he said, pointing in the other directions.

"West," Castor said, laughing to himself like that was a good joke. He hurried over to a paper on the wall and scratched out the words, muttering them to himself. Jesse didn't even want to guess how he would spell them.

"So Westlund—the giants' main settlement, I'd guess—is in the east," Owen said. "Probably past the swamps altogether and in the Wastelands. No wonder we never found it!" He paused. "If it's in the east, why is it called *West*lund?"

"Their word for the direction west isn't the same as ours," Jesse reminded him.

Castor had finished his task and turned his attention back to his guests.

"So, this man Gideon," Jesse said. "Did he go to Westlund willingly?"

"Yes, Gideon go to Westlund," Castor repeated. "He is a. . . ." He struggled for the word. "He make this." He pointed to the glass around the lamp on his desk.

Since Castor seemed to have run out of things to talk about, Jesse decided to get a closer look at the bookshelf. All of the books were crammed onto the top four shelves. Only the lower two were within Jesse's reach.

Castor noticed Jesse staring at the bottom shelves. "Water," he said miserably. He picked up a book from the top of a stack on a writing desk and showed them the damage the rising water had done to it, presumably before he had emptied the shelves.

"So, our friend can read and write," Jesse said to himself. For some reason—probably the broken Amarian—he assumed the Westlunders were uneducated.

"Yes, I read," Castor said, excited to hear words he recognized. He tapped the open book in the center of the desk. "I write a book of. . . ." He paused, thinking. A look of frustration came to his face.

Suddenly, he slammed the book shut, clearly frustrated. "Words! I no have your words for say what I have here." He pointed to his head.

Jesse tried to imagine how hard it would be to communicate with such a limited vocabulary. Once, in Da'armos, he had been among people who did not speak his language, but then he had traveled with Samar, an able interpreter who spoke both Amarian and Da'armon fluently. *We take the ability to talk to others for granted,* he realized.

Jesse walked over to the desk and flipped pages of the book. There were lines and lines, in fairly small print for someone so large with long, complicated-looking sentences. While Castor was forced to talk like a small child in Amarian, he was probably a scholar in the language of Westlund.

Within the pages, Jesse found a diagram of a very familiar city. "This is Lidia, isn't it?"

Castor nodded. "Lidia," he repeated. "Book of Lidia and Westlund." He looked pleadingly at Jesse. "Word please?"

"Boring?" Owen suggested.

Jesse hit his arm. "You'll confuse him," he muttered. He glanced back at Castor's book. There were maps, but it was more than a book of geography. The Westlund letters were slightly different than those in the Amarian alphabet, but Jesse recognized some of the words: Amarias, Terenid, and in a list on one page, Jardos, Hyram, and Vincent. There was a neat block paragraph about each of them.

"History?" Jesse guessed, trying to supply Castor's missing word. "Things that happened a long time ago?"

Something about Jesse's definition seemed to stick, and Castor nodded. "Book of history. History of Watchers, most."

That led to a new question. "What do the Watchers do?"

Castor just stared at him. "We watch."

"Very helpful, thank you," Owen said sarcastically.

"You're welcome," Castor said, almost automatically. Gideon may have left out some grammar lessons, but he had clearly taught Castor his Amarian manners.

There was a loose page in the book. Its thin, spidery script contrasted with the thick, strangely formed letters of the pages around it. And it was in Amarian.

"It's the inscription from the entranceway," Jesse said, taking it out of the book. "Only with the missing pieces filled in."

Three give their all
For Lidia's call.
Son of Amarias,
Lidias son,
Son of Westlund
Join as one.

Their sacrifice
Of greatest price
Reveals the key
To Lidia's wealth
And destiny.

Beneath the inscription were longer lines in the same handwriting.

These are the words of Parros deGuardi, unfortunate explorer from District Two, now among the Vanished, along with my company. This, as far as I could gather, is what the lines of the damaged Lidian inscription ought to read, although I have no way of knowing for certain. I speak limited Westlundish, but I have attempted to communicate these lines and their probable interpretation to the Watchers, the giants who live under the city and search it every night to find any passing travelers.

"So that's what they are," Jesse muttered. It made sense. All of the rumors of people disappearing in the swamp….

"I can't believe that no matter where you are, you can find something written down," Owen said, flopping onto Castor's lone chair.

Jesse ignored him and kept reading.

As I understand it, the lines refer to some sort of ritual that must be performed in the presence of three people, one from each of the ancient people groups surrounding Lidia.

Whatever that ritual might be, it would allow the discovery of the fabled Lidian treasure, long lost to the ages, which drew me to this godforsaken swamp.

Jesse remembered the stone carving around the entranceway's border: "Not all that is missing is gone." Could the legend of treasure really be true?

Tomorrow the moon is full. I have chosen to go to Westlund rather than remain in this underground prison. All in my company have chosen similarly (though one perished in our initial struggle with the Watchers in the ruins). I will learn a trade, rebuild a life and perhaps, with time and research, uncover the secret of the Lidian treasure at last.

So, that was what Castor had been trying to tell them. His tutor, Gideon, had chosen the same fate as Parros deGuardi. All who entered the ruins were captured. Those who struggled died, but those who surrendered were allowed to live as citizens in Westlund.

That gave Jesse hope. If he and two others performed this mysterious ritual, they might be freed. Maybe they could even persuade the Westlunders to let them go. Castor, at least, seemed reasonable.

Owen yawned loudly.

"Tired?" Castor asked, giving him a strange look. Then he got a look of realization on his face. "Yes. You sleep at night. Watchers watch at night. Sleep at day."

He threw open the door to the other room. "Sleep, son of Amarias and son of Lidia," he said, patting Owen on the head.

Castor's bed was the only item in the room, besides a trunk at the bed's foot. Owen jumped up on it, bouncing around.

"I come back at day," Castor said. He set their oil lamp, still lit, on the trunk and backed toward the door. "Goodnight. We wait for circle moon."

Almost as soon as he closed the door, Owen stopped jumping. "As soon as he and his Watcher friends leave, we're getting out of here."

"Quiet," Jesse said, glancing at the door. "He'll hear you."

"He doesn't speak Amarian," Owen said.

"He's just as intelligent as you," Jesse countered. "And he can understand more than you think."

"Fine," Owen lowered his voice. "We can bring one of his kitchen knives and pry the others' chains off, then run up the stairs and out of the city."

"You forgot one thing," Jesse said. "Even if we could free the others, which I doubt, we can't escape. The giants are leaving the tunnels…but they're going up into the city, probably to all of the gates. You think they'd just let six people leave?"

"So we split up," Owen said, shrugging. "That way they won't spot us so easily."

"And what if even one person gets caught again?" Jesse said.

Owen didn't say anything.

"Besides," Jesse continued, "if we're the two sons they've been missing, they might let us go after whatever ritual we have to participate in."

"What are you talking about?" Owen demanded.

Jesse quickly explained what he had read in the book. "You never told me you were from Lidia," Owen said.

"I'm not," Jesse said, blinking. "I'm from District One."

"Well, so am I," Owen said. He yanked off his shoes and threw them on the floor. "But Castor-the-giant called us the 'son of Amarias and son of Lidia.' So one of us has to be Lidian."

Jesse groaned, reaching up to touch Barnaby's token, the one the two giants had gotten so excited about. "The Kin," he said. "Of course! They live near the swamps, and they act like their own tiny country. They must be descendants of the Lidians, and the giants saw Barnaby's pendant and assumed I was Lidian."

"Well, you'll have to tell them in the morning," Owen said, flopping down on the bed and burrowing under the blanket. "Right now, I'm ready for sleep."

Jesse took off his wet shoes and socks and set them out to dry on the chest. He felt guilty getting into Castor's bed with tar caked all over his clothes, but he didn't have anything to change into.

Castor's words came back to him: "We wait for circle moon." If Jesse remembered correctly, the full moon would come soon. He closed his eyes. Hopefully, by then they would be out of Below-Lidia alive.

Chapter 13

When Jesse woke up without Owen beside him, he groaned, immediately coming up with a list of the trouble Owen could be getting into without him. *Maybe the Westlunders took him to the prison. Or maybe he went back to Lidia and is hiding in some suit of armor in the palace. Or he's in the crypt, drawing pictures on the walls.*

The last place he expected him to be was sitting in Castor's front room, talking animatedly with the giant. But that's exactly what he was doing, although he stopped as soon as he saw Jesse.

"What are you doing?" Jesse demanded. Something about Owen's upturned nose and bright smile made him always look mischievous, but he could tell Owen was struggling to hold back a laugh.

"Having Amarian lessons," Owen said cheerfully. "Listen!"

"Jesse look ugly this morning!" Castor said politely.

"Does he know what that means?" Jesse asked Owen, who just shrugged.

Castor looked from Jesse to Owen. Despite Owen's

innocent smile, he seemed to understand exactly what had happened. "Owen says means hello," he said. "But no?"

"See," Jesse said to Owen. "Castor's just met you, and he can already see through your innocent act."

Owen made a face at him. "At least we saved you some breakfast."

Even the mention of the word made Jesse realize how empty his stomach was. A day with nothing but fruit to eat had taken its toll. "Where is it?"

"No," Castor said, shaking his head. "First, water. Jesse is—."

"Ugly," Owen insisted.

Castor ignored him, waiting for Jesse to give him the word.

"Dirty," Jesse said.

Castor nodded. "Jesse, please wash in water." He presented Jesse with a basin of warm water. There was a large sponge floating in it. Jesse soaked it and wiped at his arm. The water in the basin soon turned a dingy brown, but flecks of tar still stuck stubbornly to Jesse's arms.

He pointed to them and asked, "Can I have…something else?" Castor inspected the tar and nodded, disappearing into the bedroom and returning with a coarse bristled brush. Jesse gritted his teeth and scrubbed, managing to get most of the caked tar off of his face, neck, and arms.

When he set the brush down and turned around, Castor frowned. "Jesse, you are…." Again the word seemed to escape him. He pointed to Jesse's skin, glowing pink after the scrubbing.

"It's called clean," Owen said. "Something Jesse hasn't been in a long time."

Castor shrugged, dismissing whatever had bothered him. "Breakfeast," he said, pointing to a bowl on the table. Jesse didn't correct the mispronunciation, although the sticky, gray-brown contents of the bowl didn't look like any kind of feast. *At least Owen managed to teach Castor one useful word.*

He took a cautious spoonful, and the food burnt his tongue so much he wasn't sure how he felt about it. The second spoonful was better, and he could tell it was a kind of porridge that would have been tasteless except for the bits of yellow fruit mixed in. Jesse recognized the fruit from the vineyard outside the palace. *So that's who harvested the fruit. And who kept the rope in the well in good repair, and created the smoke, and left a hundred other small signs of life in the abandoned ruins. The Watchers.*

"Owen teach me more Amarian words," Castor said.

"Good," Jesse said, giving Owen a stern look. "I hope the rest of them were defined correctly."

"Most of them," Owen said. He grinned. "Well, some of them. I taught him a few phrases on my own. But the rest were just words he pointed to from some book."

That made Jesse pause, a spoonful of porridge halfway to his mouth. "A book in Amarian?"

"This book," Castor said, setting a heavy book on the table next to Jesse.

Jesse's spoon clanked to the table. It was the Forbidden Book. He would recognize it anywhere. "Where did you get this?" Jesse demanded. He opened the cover and fingered the wax seal of the red dragon.

"From Amarian boy in prison," Castor said.

Silas. Jesse wondered how much of a fight he had put up before Castor got the book away from him.

"What say the book?" Castor asked. It was a thick, heavy volume, but he held it easily in one hand.

Jesse hesitated. "Do you understand the word evil, Castor?"

He nodded. "Right, wrong. Night, morning. Good, evil." Gideon had clearly spent a day teaching Castor opposites.

"The people who wrote this book were evil," Jesse said. "They tried to kill us and many others like us."

"Wait," Owen said, "it's that book you were talking about?" He reached for it, nearly spilling what was left of Jesse's porridge. "Let me see my picture!"

His hand froze halfway there when a loud voice in Westlundish stopped him. He and Jesse both looked up. There, in the doorway, was an unsmiling Westlunder, with a small silver hatchet strapped to his side.

"Head Watcher," Castor muttered to them. "He is...." Words failed him again. "Not evil, but...." He shrugged.

It struck Jesse that the contrast between good and evil was very clear, at least in the bare definition of the words. In real life, though, things became more complicated. It was much harder to describe people who were thoughtlessly careless, or who were friendly but discriminated against a group of people, or who were simply lazy and selfish. *Maybe all of us are a mixture of evil and good*, Jesse thought. *Some just choose evil more often than good.*

The Head Watcher seemed to be one of those people. Jesse could see a hardness in his eyes, and though he could not understand the words the man barked out at Castor, he could recognize the superior tone of his voice.

"Head Watcher says we come with him to Gathering," Castor translated. "Gathering is every circle moon, before we change with other Watchers from Westlund."

So it's a kind of shift schedule, Jesse realized. *Some of the Watchers stay underground in Lidia for a month, and then the other half comes from Westlund to replace them.*

The Head Watcher left without waiting for them to agree to come. Jesse was sure they had no choice.

To his surprise, Castor led them to the prison, where Parvel, Rae, Silas and Barnaby were still chained to the wall. There were eleven other giants waiting, crowded in groups against the wall, as if trying to stay as far away from the prisoners as possible.

The instant the Head Watcher entered, all talk ceased. He strode to the middle of the room, turned to face them and began a speech in Westlundish, barely pausing for Castor to translate.

"He says that in past days, there is much rain. Below-Lidia has much water come up," Castor said, struggling to keep up with the Head Watcher. "And man alone in city kill two Watchers in week past."

The Guard Rider. It had to be.

"We need do something before more happens wrong," Castor continued.

It was superstitious, Jesse knew, to believe that some kind

of ritual will stop the rain from coming into the tunnels. *It's much more likely there's a leak somewhere that needs to be fixed.*

"He says also of the words on the wall, of the Lidian treasure. We Watchers look and wait for the treasure many years." Castor paused, his eyes focused and hands tense at his side. "We all are sons of Westlund. In past days, Watchers find many sons of Amarias. But now we find first son of Lidia."

Jesse didn't think now was the time to tell him that he wasn't Lidian. Castor was struggling so much that Jesse thought he might start to sweat from the effort of translating.

Then the Head Watcher looked straight at Jesse and Owen, still speaking. Jesse didn't like the look in his eyes as he put his hand firmly on the axe at his side.

"What is he saying?" Jesse hissed at Castor, who was staring at the Head Watcher in horror. Castor didn't answer.

Even Owen could tell something was wrong. "Castor," he said, and the stern voice coming from the mischievous eleven-year-old would have made Jesse laugh at any other time.

Castor looked straight at them. He had recovered his composure. "Head Watcher say to find the treasure, words say we kill three sons this next night."

"What!" Owen yelped. All of the Westlunders looked over at him.

"Castor, tell them that won't work. It doesn't make any sense," Jesse said, fighting to keep his voice calm.

"They no will listen," Castor said. His eyes, so warm and friendly just moments before, were now distant and helpless.

"You have to stop them," Owen said. "You can't just let them kill us!"

"No," Castor said. "No, I go with you." He straightened up. "I am chosen son of Westlund. 'To give my all for Lidia's call.'"

Dimly, Jesse recognized he was quoting the inscription. True, the words "their sacrifice of greatest price" did sound like death was needed to reveal the treasure.

Then he remembered. "I'm not a son of Lidia," Jesse said. "Barnaby is."

Castor pointed at the bird around Jesse's neck. "Token," he said, pointing. "All Lidians have token, like in past days."

The Head Watcher asked Castor a question, and Castor timidly answered, bowing his head. The Head Watcher jerked Jesse to the center of the room and examined him, then pronounced something with a voice of authority.

"He say you look like Hyram of Lidia," Castor translated. "Small, with…." He pointed to Jesse's leg.

A limp. Jesse recalled from the statue that Hyram had been portrayed stooping over. "I happen to share a trait with a founder of Lidia," Jesse said. "That doesn't make me a Lidian."

One of the other giants stepped forward and grabbed his arm, but with all of his strength, Jesse pushed him away, standing to face the Head Watcher. "I am not a son of Lidia," he repeated, but it didn't look like anyone in the room believed him. Some of them began to mutter amongst themselves.

Jesse looked over at Barnaby, waiting for Barnaby to speak up, to say, "He's telling the truth. He's not a Lidian, and that's not his token. It's mine."

But he never did. He didn't even look away, just stared

straight at Jesse with hard black eyes. Even Zora, perched on his shoulder, didn't move.

Jesse tried to pull himself back into the room as the giant hauled him away. "Tomas was right," he said, struggling against the giant's firm grasp. "You don't care about anyone except yourself."

Before Jesse was dragged out of the prison, he saw a flash of recognition on Barnaby's face. He hoped the mention of his brother stung—he deserved it for letting them take Jesse away.

Suddenly, the dark water flooding the tunnels seemed sinister, foreboding, like it would suck him down. Jesse leaned heavily on his staff, because his legs were weak. Then, he felt a small hand in his. It was Owen. "I don't want to die," he said.

He had never looked younger or more afraid. And Jesse had never felt more helpless. He wanted more than anything to say, "You won't. I know a way to escape," or "We'll be rescued. I'm sure of it."

Going into the swamps, Jesse had been confident he could do anything. He had been so sure of himself, now he wasn't sure of anything. He didn't want to make a promise he couldn't keep, but Owen was counting on him. Jesse tried to think of something brave, but he didn't feel brave, not any more.

Jesse remembered what Parvel once had told him, the words of Jesus, "I will never leave you or forsake you." *Parros deGuardi called these swamps "godforsaken." But it's not true. God is here.* Even though that didn't change the fact that the giants were going to kill them, Jesse felt better, stronger.

Suddenly, Jesse knew what to tell Owen. "I won't leave you," he said. "I promise. Whatever happens next, it'll happen to both of us together."

When they reached Castor's home, one of the giants stood straight and tall next to the door, posted as a guard. Jesse and Owen were shoved inside.

Before stalking away, the Head Watcher gave one last pronouncement. Jesse didn't know what he said but knew it couldn't be good.

Castor, still looking stiff and distant, translated. "The Head Watcher says, 'Three sons of the treasure, we wait for the circle moon.'"

Chapter 14

It had been nearly an hour, and Castor hadn't said a word, no matter how much Jesse and Owen pleaded and reasoned with him. He just moved back and forth across the room—which took only a few steps with his long stride—and muttered to himself in Westlundish. Every now and then, the guard at the door would poke his head in to make sure all was well.

What is the guard expecting us to do? Jesse wondered. *Burrow through the ceiling?* Leaks or no, Vincent the shipbuilder had done an excellent job. Even after hundreds of years, the tunnels were still sturdy.

Finally, Castor spoke, sitting heavily on the bench. "It is honor to die for Westlund." He didn't sound very sure of himself.

"I'll skip that honor, thank you," Owen said.

"You're welcome," Castor said dully.

"Castor," Jesse said, sitting down next to him, "you have to understand. This is not an honor. This is a disgrace. This is *wrong*."

Castor shook his head. "Jesse do not understand. In Westlund, every man is needed to…to do something—"

"Something great," Owen finished, in a small voice. Jesse looked at him, and shrugged. "Why do you think I joined the Guard?"

Castor seemed to accept Owen's translation. "I am small. Not strong." Jesse could hear the shame behind his simple words. Castor had turned red, not from anger, but from embarrassment. "All I have is words. Words and history. That is no great." Then he straightened. "But I am son of Westlund. Now, I do what I need for my people. It is honor."

"That's what the Council said to me when I joined the Youth Guard," Owen said. "No matter how good their words sounded, they were still evil. They wanted me to die."

"They want all of us to die," Jesse said. "I just never thought it would be like this." He looked up at Castor, tapping the Forbidden Book, which was still lying on the table. "You asked earlier what this was about. It was written by people like your Head Watcher. Evil people."

"Don't bother," Owen said, crossing his arms. "He can't understand you. Or he doesn't want to listen."

"Yes, he can," Jesse said, never looking away from Castor. "Castor, you have to hear me. This sacrifice is not right, just like what is written in this book is not right."

Castor looked at him for a few seconds. Obviously, Castor's mind was full of conflicting beliefs and inner struggles that he couldn't express in his limited Amarian. Maybe no one could express it, not even the greatest of scholars.

Then Castor opened the Forbidden Book. His finger moved over the text, his mouth silently forming words.

"What's he doing?" Owen demanded. "*Feeling* the words?"

"It must be easier for him to understand written Amarian than spoken," Jesse explained. "To him, we probably have an accent."

After a few pages, which Castor flipped through quickly—probably looking at the maps and pictures, Jesse decided—he abruptly stopped, an expression of deep surprise on his face.

He held the book up. "Leisel," he said, pointing to a sketch of a beautiful young woman with dark hair and piercing eyes. She was wearing a silver butterfly necklace. *The girl in the crypt.*

Clearly, Castor knew the Amarian word written underneath the portrait, Leisel, was her name. For a moment he just stared at the book, which looked small in his thick hands.

Then he did the last thing that Jesse would have expected. He began to cry. His shoulders shook, and though no tears came out of his eyes, he rocked back and forth, staring at the book and moaning quietly.

"Great. What do you do with a crying giant?" Owen asked, backing away.

"Just what you would do with an Amarian or a Lidian or anyone else," Jesse said, walking over to Castor. "You mourn with him."

They couldn't speak, at least not much. Jesse couldn't tell him the reason Leisel had died or about the hope of heaven if she believed in God. But he could stand with Castor and feel the same pain he felt.

Jesse stared at Leisel's face, realizing for the first time that every one of the hundreds of young people in the Forbidden Book had a name, a face, a story. And most of them, like Leisel's, ended tragically.

The realization made him want to tear the pages from the Forbidden Book without looking at the faces or reading their stories. It made him want to storm out of the tunnels and go to King Selen's castle in District One, raving about injustice and evil. It made him want to curl up in the corner and cry, cold and wet and confused.

Most of all, though, it made him want to ask God questions he hadn't had the courage to pray before. *How could you let them die? Are the Guard Riders stronger than you? Or do you even care?* He had felt the same sensation when he was in the tar pit, struggling and sinking deeper and deeper.

It's so senseless... hundreds of innocents dying. If I were God, I wouldn't have let them die.

If I were God.

I am not God.

The thought came to Jesse as clearly as if someone had said it out loud. He thought of Jardos, tall and proud, with his arrogant inscription, almost equated him with God. *And look what happened to him, to his great city.*

What if, somehow, all of the senseless tragedy in the Forbidden Book wasn't senseless at all? Jesse knew that's what Parvel would say. That we are limited, but God is eternal, limitlessly wise and perfectly good—that He has a plan no amount of evil can limit.

I am not God.

It wasn't an answer, not really. Jesse still didn't know why Leisel and the others had to die. It was hard, admitting that he didn't know why—that maybe only God knew, but as soon as he accepted that he felt like he'd landed on solid ground.

"It's going to be all right," Jesse said to Castor, and he really meant it.

"No," Castor said, more forcefully than Jesse had ever heard him speak. "No, not right. Wrong. Watchers watch and kill for years, waiting for sons. We kill Leisel for *treasure*."

The way he said the word, it was as if he had said the Watchers killed for dust or garbage. *And, in the end*, Jesse realized, *that's what it is. All cities fall. All treasures are lost.*

Castor stood and crossed the room in three long strides. Suddenly, he truly looked like a giant. He spoke to the guard in Westlundish. That started a long conversation, full of gestures and exclamations. Jesse heard his own name and Owen's several times.

Finally, Castor turned around, a fierce expression on his face. He slammed the door. "They give us time to go to Lidia. Find new way. Find treasure without kill."

"So once we go up to the ruins, we can escape," Owen cheered. "You're brilliant, Castor!"

"Escape?" Castor asked, turning to Jesse.

He shrugged. "Leave Lidia. Run away from the Watchers."

"No," Castor said, and his tone was more powerful and commanding than Nero's. "We escape, the Watchers find others. No more die. No more Leisels die."

"I don't care," Owen said, his voice rising in panic. "I just want to get out of here." He ran into the other room, probably to bury himself in Castor's huge blanket.

"Watchers go out with us," Castor said to Jesse. "We run, they kill us."

That was a bit of a problem. "Then what will we do?" Jesse asked.

"Find right way," Castor said firmly. And, in that moment, he looked so confident Jesse would have followed him anywhere, on any treasure hunt, no matter how crazy.

Jesse started for the doorway. "I'll get Owen."

"Owen come?" Castor asked doubtfully.

"I promised I wouldn't leave him," Jesse said firmly. "Do you know what a promise means?"

Castor nodded, then clamped his lips together, struggling. "East, south, west, north."

"I think you're a little confused," Jesse said. "Those are directions."

"No," Castor said. "They...always same. Always...."

"True," Jesse supplied. "Directions on a compass always tell the truth and never change."

Castor nodded again. "Promise means I always will, or I never will. Promise means the truth."

Then he picked up the lantern from the desk. "Owen!" he called into the other room. "Come, please. We go from here."

Six of the Watchers—Jesse noticed the Head Watcher was not among them—escorted them to the tunnel entrance. Once there, Castor gave them an order in Westlundish. Surprisingly, they nodded and went up the stairs.

"They leave to guard Lidia. They watch us." Castor said.

Just then, something shrieking darted past Jesse in the

near-darkness. Jesse ducked, shielding his face with his hands. *I didn't know there were bats down here.*

But, when he peeked out from under his arms, he saw that his assailant was not a bat. There, perched on an outcropping of rock, was Zora. "So, you finally left Barnaby," Owen said. "Good choice. We'll take you out of here." He reached for her. She scrabbled away, eyeing him warily.

"She certainly doesn't like you," Jesse said, shaking his head.

"It might have something to do with a certain incident at a tar pit outside the swamp," Owen admitted.

Jesse made a mental note to ask him for that story later. It sounded entertaining.

Castor didn't seem to care much about Zora. He pointed to the faded carving on the wall, holding the lantern close to it. "Wrong," he said. "Must be wrong. Have to say why to Watchers. Please, find what to say, Jesse?"

Jesse was struck again with how expressive Castor's eyes were, saying more than his limited words ever could. This time, they were pleading with him to find something wrong with the inscription, something that would mean the three of them wouldn't have to die. He knew it was the only way to convince the Watchers.

"If only I had Parros deGuardi's paper," Jesse muttered. He briefly considered going back to get it, but that would waste the short amount of time they had.

"Amarian deGuardi," Castor said, clearly remembering the name from his book. "Wrote words from stones."

"What a job," Owen said. "Sounds fascinating."

Jesse shot him a look. "We need to compare deGuardi's translation, his words, with this."

"To find wrong," Castor said. "Careful look at words. I know words."

"But we don't know the words," Jesse said, pointing to the chipped paint. "See? Especially at the bottom, there are so many missing that deGuardi could have easily made a mistake."

"Not this words," Castor said. "Words of Amarian deGuardi." Then he began reciting the translation, slowly and carefully.

Three give their all
For Lidia's call.
Son of Amarias,
Lidia's son,
Son of Westlund
Join as one.
Their sacrifice
Of greatest price
Reveals the key
To Lidia's wealth
And destiny.

These are the words of Parros deGaurdi, unfortunate explorer from District Two, now among the Vanished, along with. . . ."

"That's enough," Jesse said, still slightly stunned. *He memorized the entire thing, even when he didn't know what most of the words meant.* "Thank you."

As usual, Castor was ready with a quick, "You're welcome."

"That deGuardi got us into a lot of trouble," Owen grumbled. "The Head Watcher is sure he meant all three of us would have to die. Even if that's what he was saying, how could he be sure he wrote everything down right? Some words are almost all gone."

He had a point. Jesse looked at the original inscription.

Thre g v the r all
For Li ia's cal
S n of Ama as
Lidi son
Son of Wes l d
J in as o
Th r sa if ce
O gr es pr
eals t e key.
To L a' we l
nd t y

As Jesse stared at the old, faded words, an idea came to him.

"What if deGuardi was close, but not exact in the translation?" Jesse said, more to himself than Castor or Owen. He pointed to the middle line. "There's a space after 'Join,' but deGuardi translated it as a full word. What if the line actually reads, 'Joined as one'? And what if this," he pointed to the first line, "is really 'Three *gave* their all'?"

"So?" Owen said.

Jesse stepped as close as he could to the wall, carefully rubbing a layer of ash away. "'Conceals the key,'" he said, his voice rising in excitement. "Not 'reveals.'"

"Conceals?" Castor asked.

Owen made a motion like he was hiding the words, glancing around to see if anyone was watching. "Conceal," he said.

Castor nodded, although Jesse wasn't sure if he understood exactly.

"The ritual won't reveal the key," Jesse said slowly. "The key is concealed."

"Where?" For once, Castor's Amarian was enough for the task at hand.

"With the three who *gave* their all," Jesse said, using his new translation. "A son of Lidia, Amarias, and Westlund. One from each of the ancient people groups surrounding Lidia. History."

"History," Castor said, his eyes lighting up. "Three. Jardos, Hyram, and Vincent."

Again, Jesse felt ashamed that he was surprised Castor could figure out the riddle so quickly. Even without a strong grasp of Amarian, he was capable of very advanced thinking. Jesse got the sense that in his own language and among his own people, Castor was far more intelligent than he was.

"Don't tell me," Owen said, sighing loudly. "We're going back to those statues of dead people."

"Yes, we are," Jesse said, "because those dead people could save your life."

Castor was already climbing the stairs that led to the wine cellar. Zora, cawing loudly, followed them, still staying a distance away from Owen.

"Wait," Jesse said, and Castor paused, looking curiously back to see what the delay was. "The words in the stone said that one of the three statues had to be a son of Westlund."

"One is," Castor said. He frowned and corrected himself. "Was." He turned again. "Hurry, please. Night comes."

Jesse didn't need any reminder of what would happen when night came. There were still several empty compartments in the Westlund crypt. He wanted to keep it that way.

CHAPTER 15

There was no sun to be found in Lidia. Jesse had been looking forward to seeing the sun again after a day in the tunnels, but instead, a fierce storm raged in the swamps. As soon as they stepped out of the palace, raindrops advanced against them like an attacking army, driving them back and pounding a steady, even beat into the stone of the ruins. Thunder sounded, and lightning tore across the sky.

To Jesse, it seemed like all of nature was violently protesting the coming of night—the night of the circle moon, when he, Castor and Owen would be sacrificed in a ritual to find the lost treasure. That thought made him work even harder to keep up with the others as they hurried through the city to the citadel. Between Owen's boundless energy, Castor's long strides and the driving rain, it was a difficult task.

Jesse felt tense, nervous. It was the Watchers, he knew. He never saw them—even in daylight, they knew the ruins well enough to keep hidden—but he felt their eyes on him.

Zora had stayed with them only a few moments after they left the palace. Even in the heavy rain, she had managed to fly away, letting out one parting screech as she fled Lidia forever. Jesse wished they could leave so easily. *But even if we could fly, we couldn't leave the others behind.*

"North," Castor said, pointing toward the street that led to the citadel, sounding proud that he remembered his new Amarian word. Although Jesse was sure Owen, at least, remembered exactly how to get to the citadel, they let Castor lead the way.

By the time they were inside the main hall, Jesse was soaked to the skin. *At least my clothes are cleaner*, he reasoned, though the thought was not very comforting.

"Son of Westlund," Castor said proudly, pointing to the statue of Jardos, sovereign of Lidia. "King for ten and ten and six years." Apparently, he had only been taught numbers up to ten.

Now Jesse realized that the impressive height of the statue hadn't been an illusion caused by its position on a pedestal. Compared to Vincent and Hyram, Jardos was exceptionally tall. Suddenly, other details began to fall into place in Jesse's mind. The furniture in the palace—the tall chairs, the massive table—had been sized for a Westlunder. The height of the tunnels also made sense. After all, a giant had been the one to commission them.

That left only one question. "Why was a Westlunder the king of Lidia?" Jesse asked.

"No," Owen said, before Castor could try to explain it. "We don't have time for that. We'll get Castor's book translated and read all about it later. Once we escape certain death."

"Jardos was my father father father father father," Castor said. "Is why I was chosen as son…as the son of Westlund."

That made sense to Jesse. Jardos was tall, yes, but he was much shorter than some of the Watchers, just like Castor. *Maybe Jardos tried to pass as a Lidian,* Jesse theorized. *Or maybe he was exiled from Westlund and banded together with the people living near the swamps, and eventually emerged as their leader.*

There was a story there. He could see it in the gleam of excitement and pride in Castor's eyes when he looked at the statue.

Focus, he commanded himself. *Find the treasure.* He paused. *Unless….*

Owen ran over and pulled one of the axes on the wall. His thin arms strained until it came loose, nearly throwing him backward. He dragged it over to the base of Jardos' statue. "Maybe the statue is just a layer of stone around a lump of gold."

Castor yelped and grabbed the handle of the axe, jerking it away from Owen.

"Not you too," Owen said, rubbing his sore hands. "They're *dead.* They wouldn't want us to die too, not for a stupid treasure."

"What if there is no treasure?" Jesse asked, finally putting his thoughts into words.

"There *is* treasure," Castor insisted. "History—many people speak of the treasure."

"But that could be nothing but a legend."

"Legend?"

Jesse sighed and tried to think of a way to explain it. "A legend is a story that isn't true."

"All legends have true," Castor said, frowning. "No, truth. All legends have truth. Small truth, large truth. But first people say truth, and truth makes into legend."

"Not always," Owen said. "My sister told me the old lady who lived next to us turned into a monster every night and ate goats. None of *that* was true."

But Jesse was starting to realize what Castor was saying. Jesse had thought the legend of disappearing travelers was foolish, but it was based on truth. Parvel had thought the giants didn't exist, but the stories about them, though wildly exaggerated, were based on truth.

"Besides," Owen said, "the other giants only let us out so we could find the treasure on our own, without a sacrifice. They're probably watching us right now. We can't get away. This is our only chance."

Jesse nodded. Owen was right.

"Great," Owen said, trying to grab the axe back. Castor wouldn't let him have it.

"Let's search the statues first," Jesse said. "If we have to, we'll cut one open, but this is history, Owen."

"Apparently, that's pretty important around here," Owen grumbled. "More important than my life." But he jumped up and grabbed Jardos' leg, clambering up the side of the statue and tapping on it here and there. Castor knelt and ran his hands along the base.

Jesse felt himself drawn back to the inscription. He read the lines again and again. There was nothing unusual about them, except that the first line was 'High was my reach,' instead of the more common expression, "long was my reach." *Maybe a reference to his unusual height and Westlunder background.*

He eventually started searching what he could reach of the statue from the ground. Unlike Owen, he couldn't climb very well even with his staff. That left him Jardos' feet and legs to examine.

"What are we looking for?" Owen asked. "A secret message in his beard that says, 'Look for the treasure here?' I thought the Westlunders searched this whole city. No hiding place would last through all that…unless it's *inside* these statues."

"A key," Castor said.

"Yes," Jesse said. "These three are supposed to conceal the key to the treasure, or the treasure's location. We don't know which."

Castor just laughed. "Jardos conceals…concealed the key for years. No Watcher finds….finded?"

"Found," Jesse corrected. "No Watcher found the treasure."

"No Watcher found the key. *This key*!"

Jesse stuck his head around the corner and saw Castor holding up a delicate silver key. He pointed to a thin, barely noticeable crack at the base of the statue, in the back. Owen jumped down from Jardos to see and immediately ran to the next statue. "It was here all along," Jesse said, shaking his head. "All these years, and the key really did lie with the three founders of the city. The three sons."

"Vincent's got one too," Owen said, already crawling over the second statue. He popped up, swinging the key around his finger. "Those Lidians were smarter than I thought."

Castor went ahead of Jesse to the third statue, the one of Hyram. Instead of crouching to get the last key, though, he gestured to Jesse. "Find the key, Jesse, son of Lidia."

"I told you, I'm not a son of Lidia, Barnaby is," Jesse said. He bent down anyway, feeling along the back of the statue.

"The boy with the bird?" Castor demanded. Then his face registered understanding. "The bird on the token. The same?"

Jesse came out with the third key in his fist. "I told you that already. It was all a misunderstanding. I'm as Amarian as Owen is."

"I thinked you was not say the truth," Castor admitted. Jesse tried not to wince at his attempt at grammar. "When Watchers say they will kill you, you lied, I thinked."

"No. It was true," Jesse said.

"Well, now that we've got that cleared up, what are we going to do?" Owen demanded, walking to the coat of arms in the center of the tower's floor. Jesse and Castor joined him. "We have three keys. What do they unlock?"

Suddenly, Jesse felt deflated. Owen was right. They were back where they started. He stared at the key. In its handle was a scrolled *S*, the same design as the three *S's* in the crest beneath them. Sovereign, Scholar, Shipbuilder—the three founders of Lidia. But there was no clue about where the treasure they had accumulated was hidden.

Castor sat down on the tile floor in front of Jardos, as if waiting for his ancestor to speak and give them guidance. Jesse sat down next to him, reading the poem on the base again.

"There's nothing there," Owen said, standing over him.

"We already figured out why Lidia was called 'the Noble Hill.' It's because of the tunnels."

"Noble Hill," Castor said. "'*Those who dare to pay the cost will shout this from the sky: Not all who vanish are truly lost. The Noble Hill will never die!*'"

Jesse recognized the quote from the stone inscription in the tunnels. "Interesting," he said. "In my mind, I thought it said, 'Those who dare to pay the cost will shout this *to* the sky.' But 'from?' That doesn't make sense."

"It's poetry," Owen said. "It's not supposed to make sense."

"Not here," Jesse said. "Every word is important. Every word has truth."

And so does every legend.

"The Giants' Staircase," Jesse said. "Owen, you were sent here to look for the Giants' Staircase. Where did that legend come from? What truth was it built on?"

"Maybe it's the staircase that leads into the tunnels," Owen tried. "That was a pretty important staircase."

"No, it can't be," Jesse said. "The legend clearly talks about a staircase that reaches to the heavens. Like the underground carving said, 'from the sky.'" He pointed to Jardos. "This poem talks about Jardos' reach being 'high'—maybe a reference to some sort of tower or staircase."

"This tower?" Castor asked.

"Three stories isn't exactly reaching to the sky," Jesse said, frowning. "And this would be one of two places the Westlunders would have looked first: the citadel and the palace."

"Well, we're in the middle of a swamp," Owen said. "It's

not exactly the best place to build a tower. It would sink into the ground. Besides, if it existed, we'd be able to see it over the trees."

"That's it!" Jesse cried, jumping up so quickly his bad leg throbbed, but he didn't care. "Owen, you've done it. It has to be."

"Great. Cut me in on part of the treasure," Owen said, clearly not convinced.

"Owen, what's the tallest structure in Lidia? One that reaches to the skies?"

But it was Castor who answered. "The Lidia Tree."

CHAPTER 16

Even Jesse, with his poor sense of direction, could find what Castor called the Lidia Tree. Visible from any point in the city, it was an impressive sight, especially when a streak of lightning seemed to carve its dark silhouette into the sky.

Castor pointed to the swamp beyond the city walls. "Smoke," he said.

"Clouds," Jesse corrected. He could see why Castor would confuse the two words. These clouds were as dark as any thick smoke. *But no one—not even Captain Demetri and his party—could make a fire in this weather.*

Jesse kept his hand on the key in his pocket, afraid it would somehow slip out and fall into the ancient sewer grates. *The Westlunders searched the whole city—every obscure hiding place—for the treasure, and it was in the most obvious location of all. Right above them.*

Standing underneath the tree, Jesse felt as he had expected to feel when seeing one of the Westlund giants: small, powerless and insignificant.

The tree looked older than the ruins, older even than the swamp spreading out around it. It had seen generations come and go and kingdoms rise and fall. Even with the few scars and burn marks on its outer layers, the tree had hardly been touched by the destruction of Lidia. Bare branches stretched out over the ruins, like a mourner dressed in black. The tree had been dead for many years, though its deep roots kept it standing firm.

If Jesse were right, the reason the mighty tree had died was not from disease or disaster. Not a natural disaster, anyway. It had been hollowed out to hide the legendary treasure of Lidia.

"But there's nothing here," Owen said. He had run all the way around the trunk as soon as they reached it. "No way to get inside."

"I doubt they would place a large lock right at the base where all could see it," Jesse said, trying to sound confident. *If I'm wrong....* "It must be up higher."

Now he realized why the Westlunders hadn't found the hiding place in the tree. The branches started just above Jesse's head, but the tree was so wide and solid it would take many days of labor to fell it.

We don't have many days, he realized. Somehow, he doubted that the giants, especially the Head Watcher, would be impressed by a vague idea about treasure inside a tree. He looked up at it until rain drenched his face. There were no signs of a lock, a door or anything unnatural.

"We must climb," Castor shouted, over a sudden rumble of thunder.

"I knew I liked you!" Owen cheered.

Just looking up at the tree made Jesse feel sick. With the wind and the rain, it couldn't be safe. Then again, he doubted a ritual sacrifice would be very safe either. "Castor…" he began.

"Owen first, then Jesse," Castor said. He held up his key. It looked very small in his large hand. "Three keys. Three sons must climb Lidia Tree."

Jesse was about to protest that he wasn't even one of the sons in the poem when Castor picked Owen up with a grunt of effort, placing him on the lowest branch. "Here I go," Owen said, scrambling to the next.

"Be careful," Jesse warned. *But that looked simple enough.* He couldn't deny that he wanted to see the Lidian treasure for himself. *Besides, Owen isn't a very thorough searcher.*

Jesse remembered the words of the poem: "Those who dare to pay the cost will shout this from the sky…." *Do I dare to pay the cost?*

Yes. For Silas, Rae and Parvel, I will climb.

"Jesse?" Castor asked, waiting.

Jesse took a deep breath and set down his staff. It would be of no use in a tree. "All right."

It was a strange sensation, being lifted through the rain into the shelter of the dense tree branches. Castor's grip was firm, but not threatening. Still, Jesse was glad when he was set down on solid wood. Even though the tree had stopped sending nutrients to its branches, they were still thick and strong where they met the trunk.

Owen was moving far too quickly for Jesse's liking. The

boy was already two stories high. "The branches are wet," Jesse reminded him, speaking loudly to be heard over the rain. "And they're brittle at the ends."

"I'm not going to the ends," Owen said, jumping over to another branch with an ease that made Jesse wince. "That's not where the lock would be."

Suddenly, the branch shook wildly, and Jesse grabbed at the trunk. Castor, his powerful arms straining, was pulling himself up.

"You could have warned us," Jesse grumbled. Already, the ground looked very far away.

"I'm sorry," he said, but his face gave him away. *He's having as much fun as Owen.* "Go!" he said, pointing.

To his surprise, Jesse found he was able to pull himself up by his arms, at least to the next branch. A month in the Youth Guard had made him stronger. Still, he let Owen dart around the width of the tree, knocking on the wood and feeling it carefully for any cracks. *No sense in taking unnecessary risks.*

He almost laughed, realizing how much like Silas he sounded. They were not with him, but they had left their impact: Silas' caution, Parvel's love of history, Rae's spirit. He had missed not having them with him for the past few days, but he had unknowingly picked up some of their traits in their absence.

"Nothing yet," Owen said. "Higher?"

"Higher," Castor said, in a tone much more confident than Jesse could have managed.

The higher they went, the more exposed Jesse felt. The thunder seemed to get louder, the lightning closer—like the fury of the heavens was closing in on them. They began to feel the tree sway, as the wind beat against the narrower middle branches. It was as if they were climbing into the storm.

But, although Jesse was surprised at what he could do, using only his arms and his good leg, each branch became harder to get to. Once, he felt his foot slip, and he dangled from his arms until he found another foothold.

He leaned against the trunk, clinging to a branch and tried to slow his heartbeat. The top was still a long distance away. "This is as far as I can go," he managed. The rain had slowed a little, but he clung to the tree, cold, wet and exhausted.

"We're not there yet," Owen protested from a few branches above him.

"We don't even know where 'there' is," Jesse countered. "There may not be anything up here at all. What's the sense in getting killed for that?"

"But—"

"Jesse is right," Castor said. "I and Owen climb—say if we find…what?"

He had a point. They weren't exactly sure what they were looking for. "A knothole disguising a lock," Jesse said. "Or a panel of some kind that looks like it's hiding a lock." "Or just a lock," Owen said.

"Well, yes," Jesse said. "But I doubt it would be that easy."

"You say this *easy*?" Castor grunted. Jesse noticed that although Castor had managed to go a few branches higher than Jesse, he was breathing hard. Probably sweating too, although they were all so soaked by the rain it was impossible to tell.

"Well, here it is," Owen insisted. "A lock with three keyholes." Jesse tried to look up. It was better than looking down, anyway. Owen had his legs tucked around a high branch, close to the top of the tree. He was eye-to-eye with something that, even in the dark, gleamed silver.

"That's it?" Jesse asked doubtfully. "I thought it would be hidden better."

"It's three stories up in a tree, hidden by branches," Owen pointed out. "Who's going to see it here?"

It was a good point. Apparently, the Westlunders hadn't, even though they had searched the entire city for the treasure.

"My key works!" Owen cried.

Jesse felt like cheering. *Maybe this is it. Maybe we've really found the lost Lidian treasure.* He smiled as he recalled the second line in the underground inscription. *'Not all that is missing is gone.' Not gone for good, anyway.*

"Now mine," Jesse said. He struggled to stand, clutching a branch tightly with one hand, and with the other passing his key to Castor, who easily reached up to Owen. There was a pause, and Jesse winced as a roll of thunder shook the ground.

The key turned. "Give me yours, Castor," Owen called. Castor did, and Owen turned the third key in the lock.

Then Owen pulled on the keys like he would pull on a handle, and a door came away from the tree, a thick slab of wood nearly as tall as Owen. "There's an opening inside!" he crowed.

But, instead of hurrying in like Jesse thought he would, Owen looked down. "Let's go," he said.

Jesse glanced up, measuring the distance. *It's not so far....*

Then he looked down. "I'm staying here," he called up to Owen. "Go in without me."

Instead, Castor lowered himself until he was on the branch next to Jesse. It shook under his weight, but he didn't flinch. "Come, Jesse," he said. "With us." When Jesse still didn't answer, he added, "Promise."

What Jesse wanted to say was, "When I promised not to leave him, I didn't mean climbing up a tree in a storm."

But then he remembered what Castor had said about the compass: "Promise means I always will, or I never will." *No matter what.*

Besides, think how Rae will mock me if she finds out I came so close to the treasure, but stopped short.

"Help me," Jesse said, grabbing onto Castor's hand.

"In Amarian, good to say please," Castor said, looking down his nose at him.

"Please help me," Jesse amended. Gideon, whoever he was, had certainly been careful to teach Castor manners.

Castor grinned. "Yes. We go together. The three sons."

Slowly, carefully, they made their way up, with Castor leading the way and pulling Jesse up after him. A few times, Jesse was afraid a branch wouldn't hold their weight, but Castor stayed calm, testing the branches to find the strongest, never panicking no matter how close the thunder seemed to get.

"Stay there," Owen warned, once they were just below the lock. "This branch can't hold all of us."

Jesse inspected it. He was right. It seemed like a flimsy thing. *And so far off the ground....*

He started to look down, but Castor saw and tilted his head up again. "Not down," he said firmly. "Up."

"Up" was the door, with Owen standing right in front of it.

"Wait for us," Jesse said. He pictured Owen stepping off a ledge and falling down the center of the hollow tree.

But Owen had already disappeared into the darkness. Castor jumped up to the door, shaking the branch wildly. He crawled though the opening—it was too low for him to stand—but then turned around and held out his hand for Jesse.

This is it. Jesse took Castor's hand and pushed off of his branch, grabbing the door as soon as it was within reach and finding a secure place to stand on the branch beneath it.

Before following Castor through the door, Jesse took all three keys out of the lock and put them in his pocket. *We don't want to get locked in when the door blows shut*, Silas' voice in his head told him.

Inside, they were standing on a kind of platform. The compartment in the tree was wide enough for perhaps six men. *Or, in our case, a comfortable fit for two Youth Guard members and one giant.* It was lit with rings of glowing stone around the top and bottom of the compartment.

But, as far as Jesse could see, there was nothing else there.

"Where's the treasure?" Owen demanded. He started tapping on the walls, as if the Lidians might have carved another secret compartment closer to the outside of the tree.

"Look!" Castor said. He reached a hand into the darkness. Jesse squinted and could see the vague outline of a shelf carved into the wood. Castor held up a green leather book. The silhouette of a tree was embossed on the cover in gold, and Jesse recognized a simplified version of the tree they had just climbed.

"I don't believe it," Owen said, shaking his head. "Another *book*?"

"May I see it?" Jesse asked. Castor nodded and gave it to him. Jesse sat down to be closer to the glowing stones, then opened the book. The slim volume seemed to be a list of treasures that Jesse assumed had once been stored in the Lidia tree. There were weapons, carvings, jewels and other valuables. But, more important to Jesse, were pages listing the titles of books.

So this was where the library of Lidia was hidden, Jesse thought, remembering that the other squad hadn't found any books in the city. Immediately, his disappointment became even greater. *Someone must have found it before us.*

"What does it say?" Owen asked impatiently, trying to read over Jesse's shoulder.

"Not much," Jesse said, flipping quickly to the end. *Better if he doesn't know.*

On the last page, though, the list ended. Instead, these words were written in the same careful handwriting.

> I, Nolan, last son of Hyram, seal these stairs for the last time. Who knows when they will open again? It has been nearly three months since the siege started. Our fortress, which we thought could outlast any attack, has proven to be our undoing. We can last no longer.

The keys are hidden. The city is abandoned. I will join the others soon, fleeing by way of the tunnels. Our destination is unclear. There is no place for us from now on, yet we must leave the Noble Hill.

Our current sovereign, half the man that Jardos was, both in height and in wisdom, has declared that we will return to Lidia after the Westlunders leave, and rebuild the city. He is a fool. The Westlunders will leave nothing behind. All that we have labored to create will be destroyed. Perhaps even this hiding place, so cleverly devised, will be discovered and looted. The sweat and blood of the founding generation—my father's generation—will be lost forever.

It was our own doing. We thought we would never die. Yet here are our treasures, hidden away in the symbol of our might and power: the Lidian Tree. Perhaps our greatest treasure is this warning to you who read these words, whether you are kin of Lidia or strangers here—beware the blinding pride of success and wealth.

We will not return. I leave Lidia forever.

It was sad, Jesse thought, reading the words. Nolan had been right. The descendants of the Lidians, the Kin, wandered around Amarias, never having a real home.

Wait. Jesse reread the first line again. "*I, Nolan, last son of Hyram, seal these stairs....*" All the time, he had assumed the Giant's Staircase was just a figurative term for the tree itself, one that had been transformed by centuries of legend. *But what if there is a literal staircase?*

"Of course," he said, flipping again through the pages. "There is far too much listed here to fit just in this small compartment."

"What?" Owen asked. "What is it?"

Jesse just started feeling the floorboard, searching for a familiar, straight crack. "Move to the right," he said to Castor, who looked offended. "Please," Jesse added.

Castor moved, and Jesse pried up the section of floorboard with his fingers. It came out of the floor easily, creaking on ancient hinges. "This was just the entryway," Jesse said. "The real treasure must be below."

"They like their trapdoors, don't they?" Owen observed. Jesse expected him to dive right through the trapdoor, but he didn't move. "You first," he said to Jesse's questioning look. "You found it."

"Thank you," Jesse said, but inside, his stomach was churning. Even if there were a staircase, how could he be sure it was safe? It had been built hundreds of years ago.

He knelt down and looked into the hole. Dimly, he could see the first few steps, each lit by a long, thin wedge of glowing stone. They *looked* stable enough. *But so did their city, and now it's destroyed.*

Before his worried mind could come up with more reasons not to, Jesse stood and took his first step downward, gripping the side of the platform, just in case. Nothing happened. His weight held.

Slowly, he started down the stairs, until his head had dropped past the platform level. He looked down again, and realized the stairs wound around each other. He was climbing down a spiral staircase in the center of the Lidian Tree.

And it was no rough scaffolding. The stairs were straight and perfectly fit the polished wooden railings on either side. The stone was the only light, giving the carved-out trunk a dim glow.

Once, when Castor stepped down behind him, Jesse was sure he heard the staircase groan, but Owen insisted it was only thunder. Inside the tree, the sounds of the storm seemed muffled and far away, although Jesse knew only a layer of wood separated them from it. Climbing down the staircase, Jesse felt safe somehow.

Then Jesse really did feel the stairs shift. He whirled around. Several steps above him, Owen was jumping up and down. Even in the dim light, Jesse could see a look of joy on his face. "We're rich!" he exclaimed, pointing to his left.

There, arranged neatly on shelves attatched to the wood of the tree, were the treasures Jesse had read about in the green leather book. He had been so focused on looking at where he was placing his feet he hadn't looked to either side.

Jesse reached out to the shelf next to him and picked up twin hunting dogs that looked like they were made of solid gold. "I don't believe it," he said, shaking his head. "We found it."

Each new discovery brought a shout of excitement from Owen. "Look! I found a ruby the size of my eye!" "It's a marble sculpture of some ugly man with a beard!" "Who would even wear a bracelet this heavy?"

Of course, Owen ignored the books lined up on some of the shelves, pushing past Jesse when he stopped to look at them. Jesse barely had time to scan the titles. Most were in

Amarian—Lidians, though they were a self-sustaining city within the kingdom, seemed to have spoken Amarian since early days. A few were in foreign languages. *All are treasures in their own right,* Jesse thought, and judging by Castor's incredulous face, he agreed.

The farther down they got, the wider the shelves were and the more extravagant the treasures seemed to be. Jesse's favorite was a miniature replica of a ship. Tiny letters on the hull identified it as *The Silver Crescent.* Not only were all the parts on the ship exact down to the last detail, but there were tiny clay figurines on the deck, each with unique clothing and facial expressions. Jesse turned a wooden cog to raise the sails. The rope tightened and slackened, just like on a real ship. *This could be the creation of Vincent himself,* he realized.

"I wonder how long it took to make this?" he asked, showing it to Castor. "The detail is—"

"The three sons are on coins," Owen interrupted, holding up a fistful from a small chest. He crammed them in his pocket. "The real ones, I mean. Not us. The king, the builder and that book person."

"Scholar," Jesse corrected, setting the ship down. They had to keep going. He could still see the spiral winding below them. They were only halfway through.

He stopped again only a few steps later. A rack with tiny hooks was embedded in the wall. Hanging from each hook was a delicate chain with tiny objects made of gold. Jesse leaned in closer. One was an owl with large garnets for eyes. Another was a crescent moon studded with diamonds, the third a ship's wheel that actually turned. There were others, each perfect in every detail.

They must be tokens, Jesse realized. *But far more than a simple carved object. Maybe they belonged to the royal family.*

"Look!" Castor said. Jesse turned to see him holding up a slim blue volume. "Primary Reader, Year One." He flipped it open to the first page, an illustrated picture of an anchor with a large *A* printed underneath it.

"Surrounded by treasure, and he picks up a textbook," Owen said, shaking his head.

"You're at least ready for Year Two, Castor," Jesse said, grinning.

Castor nodded seriously and picked up the entire stack of the blue readers, each one slightly thicker than the one before it.

Suddenly, Jesse realized just how long it would take to haul all of the treasure out of the tree. They would have to rig up some kind of pulley system to lower the treasure to the ground. It certainly wouldn't work to carry the treasure and climb at the same time. *And the books, at least, will have to be transported after the rain has stopped.*

As if in agreement, a clap of thunder shook the tree, one louder and harder than Jesse had ever heard. Instinctively, Jesse grabbed the railing of the staircase. He looked at the others. They seemed as afraid as he felt.

"That was close," Owen said, his wide eyes just a little worried.

"We should leave," Jesse said, but he didn't start climbing up the steps. The last thing he wanted to do was climb back down the tree in the storm. Here, at least, he felt safe, protected from the chaos outside.

But Castor was staring up the staircase, frozen. He breathed deeply. "Smoke," he said, his face empty of any expression.

"But that means—" Jesse began, trailing off when he saw Owen's terrified expression. But it was too late to protect him.

"It means the tree is on fire," Owen finished.

CHAPTER 17

What do I save?

That thought went through Jesse's mind over and over. Castor and Owen were ahead of him already, Castor taking the steps three-at-a-time. Owen had pulled up the corners of his shirt as a makeshift basket and scooped up as much treasure as he could grab.

Jesse knew Owen wouldn't be able to carry it all, not while trying to climb. *Maybe he'll throw it down from the top*, he thought, picturing gold coins falling from the sky with the rain.

For Jesse, the choice was harder. Should he take the ship? A sculpture or painting perhaps, the only remaining art of the Lidian culture? A book? If so, which one? He hardly had time to glance at the covers, much less decide which one was most important.

He knew the tree would burn quickly. He had seen dead wood catch fire before. A lightning strike could destroy an entire forest.

What do I save?

The smell of smoke was getting stronger. Jesse decided on a book. *Gold and stone might survive the fire*, he reasoned. *Paper will not.*

His eyes raced over the titles, the words blurring together until he reached one, a simple brown volume with "Holy Scriptures" written in gold. His hand froze on the cover.

Parvel's book. The book about God.

Jesse picked it up, almost reverently. For a moment, he could hear Parvel's voice again, saying, "The most important book in all of history." He had found his treasure. *And I won't let it go, even if this tree burns down around me.*

"Jesse," Castor's voice shouted from above him.

"I'm coming!" he shouted.

"Don't!" Owen's voice now, distant, but getting closer. "It's blocked. The fire started at the top. We can't—" He broke off in a fit of coughing. "We can't get out," he finished. Now he was close enough for Jesse to see him. He had dropped the treasure from his shirt.

"Think logically." Parvel's voice. So Jesse did, trying to breathe evenly and focus on the problem, not on panic. What were his options?

Charge up the burning staircase and try to make it out? *"Risky and foolish."* Silas' voice.

Give up? *"Never."* Rae's voice.

He needed time. They had no time.

"All the way down," Jesse said, limping as quickly as he could. "Maybe the rain will put the fire out before it gets to us."

But he knew it was a pointless wish. The fire would only spread faster the longer it raged, and even if no flames ever touched them, they wouldn't be able to breathe for long in the smoke-filled air.

Once they reached the stone floor at the base of the stairs, Jesse picked up an embroidered scarf from an elaborately carved chest and tied it around his mouth and nose. He handed one to Owen and turned to give one to Castor.

But Castor was busy. He had found a large axe. Judging from its size and elaborate ornamentation, it had been meant only for decoration. With a grunt of effort, he heaved the axe back and hurtled it at the tree trunk, barely making a dent.

"You'll never make it out," Jesse said. "It's too thick. If you keep struggling, you'll breathe in smoke faster."

Jesse knew Castor understood him, but he never stopped, never even slowed. He kept raising the axe, chipping away at the wood.

Jesse scanned the circular compartment around them. There was no door—of course not. If there had been one, they would have seen it when they were outside the tree. "Why isn't there another way out?" Jesse moaned.

Suddenly, Castor froze, axe in midair, sweat pouring down his face. "Not out," he said. "Down."

"What?" Owen asked.

But Jesse was already on his knees, feeling the floor with his free hand. He knew he should put the Scriptures down, but he didn't want to lose them. "Think about it, Owen. What's beneath us?"

Owen's eyes widened, and he dropped to the ground too. "The tunnels."

There would have to be a second entrance. It only made sense. How else would the Lidians have transported the treasure into the tree? It would have been difficult to haul it up, bit by bit, to the door at the top.

Jesse began feeling the glowing stone, looking for a trapdoor. Specks of ash were starting to float down. Jesse looked up. He could see the fire now at the top of the tree where the panel had been. *Nolan's warning will be lost forever now*, he thought grimly.

No. Not as long as we get out of here alive.

Castor let out a shout of triumph. Jesse looked up. He had shoved aside the carved chest, and there was another panel, with three keyholes. "Keys," he moaned, looking back toward the burning staircase.

"I have...." Jesse started to say—but his words, muffled through the scarf, were cut off by the choking smoke. Instead, he ran over and handed Castor the keys. "Owen!" he shouted.

Owen crawled over, glancing nervously at the burning stairs. Soon enough, Jesse knew, larger pieces would start to fall. They had to get out before that happened.

Castor tried to turn the keys, but his fingers were too large and clumsy. "Here," Jesse said, reaching around him. He turned all three in the lock. This time, Jesse didn't hear a click, but Castor pulled the panel open. Jesse could see nothing but darkness beneath. Castor had been right. They had found the tunnels.

When he looked over, Owen was gone. He was using Castor's axe to scrape treasure over to the opening, letting it fall down. Castor wrenched the axe from his hands. "Down," he ordered.

"But the treasure—" Owen protested.

"You are more than treasure," Castor said. "Now go down!"

Taking one last fistful of treasure, Owen jumped through the trapdoor.

"Now Jesse," Castor said, and despite his words to Owen, Jesse noticed that he was gathering books from the ground.

Jesse sat on the edge, trying to see where he would fall, but it was too dark. He stuffed the Holy Scriptures inside his shirt, feeling guilty about mistreating a sacred book.

Beneath him, Owen was shouting. *At least he's alive*, Jesse thought, but even that simple conclusion seemed to take a long time to make. The smoke was making him dizzy, clouding his senses and making him move slower.

"Go!" Castor roared.

That Jesse understood. He pushed off and fell into the darkness.

His crippled left leg hit first, and it gave out underneath him. He felt his head hit something hard, and then the shouts around him dimmed and everything else faded.

Chapter 18

When Jesse woke, he kept his eyes closed out of caution. *If I'm among the giants, it would be better if they don't know I can hear them*, he reasoned.

"I've heard of cases like this." It was Parvel's voice, worried. "Smoke inhalation stops activity in the brain."

"We have to acknowledge that he may never wake up," Silas said, his voice flat and unemotional.

"And you two have to acknowledge that none of us want to hear your medical garble or predictions of doom," Rae snapped, and Jesse had to fight back a smile. Although he was clearly among friends, he decided to wait for the conversation to finish.

"But how long can we wait?" Another voice, not so familiar. Barnaby? "The giants will leave as soon as they finish digging through the ruins of the tree, rescuing their treasures. Their stores of food will leave with them. We can't stay here forever."

"We will stay as long as it takes," Parvel said firmly. "You and Owen may leave, but we will stay."

So Owen was there too. That explained the occasional bouncing of the bed underneath him. Jesse was surprised he hadn't said anything yet.

"I should have been there," Parvel said, sounding so mournful that Jesse almost stopped the ruse right then and opened his eyes.

"Yes, so you could have gotten burned up in a lightning-struck tree," Rae said. "That would have been a great help to Jesse, I'm sure."

Again, Jesse tried not to smile. *Rae certainly knows how to ruin a serious moment.*

"He's awake," Owen said calmly.

Jesse kept perfectly still, breathing evenly. *How could he possibly know that?*

"His eyes twitched," Owen explained. "He was laughing."

"It's dark in here," Rae said. "You were imagining things."

"Yes," Jesse said. "All in your imagination." He grinned as the dim figures around the bed jumped.

All except for Owen, who folded his arms and smiled smugly. "I told you so."

He was in Castor's bedroom, surrounded by his fellow Guard members. "Where's Castor?" Jesse asked.

Barnaby, without speaking a word to Jesse, slipped out the door. *Probably wanting to avoid me as much as possible.*

"He's with the other Westlunders, searching the fallen tree," Parvel said. "Before he joined you, he managed to rescue much of the treasure on the lower level. Now, they're finding what's left from the rest of the tree."

Jesse was still focused on the first part of Parvel's words: fallen tree. The pride of Lidia, the symbol of their wealth and destiny, had finally been brought down.

"We fell out in the crypt," Owen said. "Right on top of a dead body."

Jesse shuddered. "That would explain your screams."

Owen grinned sheepishly. "I was hoping you didn't hear that."

Silas ducked out of the door and came back with one of Castor's large bowls. "Here," he said. "Eat. You need your strength back."

It was the porridge. Jesse made a face. "Don't you have any fresh bread?"

"No," Silas said, without a trace of compassion. "Be glad it's not cold."

He took a spoonful. Not bad, probably because of how hungry he was. "What next? Where do we go from here?"

"Castor thinks they'll let us go," Owen said. "Now that they have the treasure, the Watchers don't need to keep Lidia a secret from outsiders. They'll go to Westlund with the treasure and never come back. Then we can leave too. I'm ready to get away from the swamps forever."

"But your two squad members," Parvel reminded him. "They are still here somewhere, perhaps in danger. We have to find them."

"I already found them," Jesse said dully. He scooped up more porridge. "I told them everything about the king and his plan to kill the Youth Guard." He thought back to the incident in the tar pit. "Well, as much as I could, anyway. They seemed to think it was some kind of trick to pull them away from their mission."

"Leave it to Talia and Nero," Rae said spitefully. "At the training camp, they thought everything from waking up in the morning to eating dinner was a competition...and in their minds, they were always the winners."

"That's all we can do then," Silas said, shrugging. "They have fair warning. If they want to believe there is no danger, we can do no more for them."

"No," Parvel said. "We cannot abandon them."

"They want to be abandoned," Rae countered. "Anything we say will convince them even more that we are liars."

"I doubt that," Jesse said. "They have more reason to believe us now. The Guard Riders took them captive." He explained the conversation he and Owen had overheard in the ruins.

"I liked it better when Captain Demetri only had Patrol members on his side," Rae grumbled. "They, at least, were only following orders, often slowly and foolishly."

"What was the name of the other man?" Parvel asked.

"Ward," Jesse said.

Silas groaned. "I know him. He was on the Guard Council. They often came to training sessions to observe us or lectured in the teaching sessions. He was small but very shrewd. It was like, when he looked at you—"

"When he looked at you, he could see inside of you, somehow," Parvel finished. "Yes. I felt the same, Silas. He reserved a particular hatred for me...and Aleiah."

The name seemed to hang in the air for a few seconds. Jesse knew that Aleiah had been a good friend of Parvel's back in the training camp.

"I think he was happy when she died," Parvel said, bowing his head. "He gave the funeral oration. Full of words about bravery and sacrifice...but there was no mourning in his eyes."

How could a man be happy about the death of a girl only seventeen years old? Once again, Jesse felt a sense of helplessness. *What good can we do against that kind of evil?*

"Jesse!" a voice from the distance shouted, interrupting his thoughts.

The door burst open. It was Castor, ash sticking to his sweaty skin, his arms full of books. Barnaby followed him. Jesse felt guilty for his accusatory thoughts. *He was just going to get Castor.*

"You awake...." He frowned, "You *are* awake."

"And feeling better," Jesse said, although his throbbing head told him otherwise.

Barnaby held out a familiar object. "He found your staff," he said.

Jesse ran his hand along the surface. Not a scratch or a burn anywhere. He was glad now he hadn't taken it with him up the tree.

"And I found books," Castor said happily, stacking them neatly on the bed beside Jesse. "Many, many books."

"But they're all in Amarian," Jesse said.

Castor waved one of the volumes. "Primary Reader, Year One," he said proudly. "Then Year Two, and more. Six years, I will learn Amarian."

"It won't take you nearly that long," Jesse said, laughing. "You catch on quickly."

Whether or not Castor understood all of the words, he knew a compliment when he heard it. "Thank you," he said, smiling.

"You're welcome," Jesse said, and Castor grinned even wider.

"Jesse remembers manners," he said, nodding in approval.

"That's what you think," Rae said. "The rest of us know better."

Castor laughed along with everyone else, even though he probably didn't understand the joke. He was filthy and looked exhausted, but he seemed happy just to be alive.

"Oh," he said, a look of realization on his face. He hurried through the door, his footsteps falling hard on the floor.

As soon as Castor had set down the books, Parvel started looking at them with an expression of awe. Now, he hurried to Jesse's side, picking up each of the books in turn. Some of them had water damage—from falling to the flooded tunnel floor, Jesse assumed.

"These are very old books," Parvel said. "Older than even ancient Lidia. Some of these could be the only surviving copies left in the kingdom, perhaps in the world!"

"Now I know where you got it from," Owen said in triumph, poking Jesse in the side. Parvel gave him a quizzical look, but Owen just grinned at Jesse.

Jesse grinned back.

Castor had returned with a different book in his hand. He

gave it to Silas. "Yours," he said. "Sorry that they take." *The Forbidden Book.*

"I'm sorry they took it," Jesse corrected. "'It' stands in for the word 'book.'"

Jesse was sure he wouldn't understand, but Castor had clearly heard them use the word 'it' before. He nodded. "I give *it* back to you now."

"Thank you," Silas said, putting it in his pack. Jesse realized that the Westlunders had returned all their supplies, including their weapons. Rae, of course, wore her sword strapped to her side even though, underground, it was unlikely they would face danger.

Next to him, Parvel gasped. Jesse jerked his head around in alarm.

But he was only staring at one of the books in the stack. Jesse recognized the brown binding. *Of course. The Holy Scriptures.* Castor must have taken it from Jesse when he fell.

"What is it?" Rae demanded.

"Nothing important," Owen said. "He and Jesse just love books for some reason."

"No," Parvel said, his voice not entirely steady. "This is not just any book, Owen. This is—"

"The most important book of all time," Jesse finished for him. "God's book."

"God?" Castor asked, waiting for a definition.

"He managed to come up with one word that I can't define," Jesse said to Parvel, hoping for some help. "I'm not even sure I fully understand God myself."

Parvel laughed, and Jesse realized how much he had missed

that sound. "Of course not," he said, shaking his head. "Then you would be God, I imagine. And we certainly know that isn't the case."

"Yes, we do," Jesse agreed.

Castor was still waiting, so Jesse tried to think of a way to explain. "The Great Watcher," he finally said. "But not an evil one. One who is perfectly good and wise and loving."

"Love," Castor said, smiling. Clearly, he knew that word, both the bare definition and what it meant. Jesse wondered if he had a wife and family back in Westlund. They might never know.

Parvel opened the Scriptures, treating each page—warped by water damage, but still legible—with greatest care. "'In the beginning was the Word, and the Word was with God, and the Word was God,'" he read. "'He was with God in the beginning. In him was Light, and that Light was the life of men. The light shines in the darkness, but the darkness has not understood it.'"

"It's beautiful," Rae said. Jesse stared at her, but he didn't see a trace of sarcasm in her face. "Like a poem or a song."

"Do you know what it means?" Parvel asked. She shook her head.

"Nothing," Silas cut in, jerking the book away from him. "It's nothing but an ancient myth."

"No, it isn't," Jesse insisted.

"I've heard it all. My father was a priest, remember? God dying for humans—it doesn't make sense."

"Neither do most of the real things in life," Parvel said.

"Like what?" Silas challenged.

It was Castor who answered. "Love," he said. "Promises."

Jesse could only shake his head. *East, south, west, north.* For all of his limits in communication, Castor could speak up when it really mattered.

"Sacrifice," Rae added. "Loyalty." Silas shot her an accusatory look, and she shrugged. "I'm not saying I believe in God, Silas. But I believe in these things, even though they're not logical, because I've seen them."

"I don't want to talk about it," Silas snapped. He clearly realized he was outnumbered.

"Castor," Jesse said, looking at him, "can we keep this book?"

At first, Castor glanced ruefully at it, as if giving up any book was difficult for him. Then he nodded. "Yes. Please, take it."

"No," Parvel said, putting the Holy Scriptures back on the stack of books. "Keep it. Learn to read it, and tell all of Westlund about the God of its pages."

Jesse couldn't believe what he was hearing. "But Parvel," Jesse protested, "these people don't want to hear about God. Look at the way they treated us!"

"That's not for us to judge," Parvel said.

He was right, and Jesse knew it. But he didn't want to lose those words. He wanted to read them all, every page. "But you've been searching for this your whole life," Jesse said.

"No," Parvel said, shaking his head. "I've been searching for truth my whole life. And I will continue to do so." He gave Jesse a long, hard look. "They have not heard, Jesse. We cannot stay here to tell them. By taking this book away from Westlund, I would be a messenger abandoning his duty."

Jesse's finger traced the cover of the book. Then he nodded and handed it to Castor, who seemed to understand the seriousness of the gift. "I will read it," he said. "I promise."

"Now that we're done with the religion lesson," Barnaby cut in, "I believe we have some practical matters to discuss."

"Like not dying?" Owen suggested.

"You will no die," Castor said. "They will let you go. They have the treasure. Watchers will no stay here. There will no be Watchers."

He seemed almost sad about that. Jesse wondered if Castor had been a Watcher his entire life. He didn't seem to know anything else.

"It's not the Watchers I'm worried about," Jesse said. He tried to explain Captain Demetri to Castor. As far as he could tell, Castor only understood there were some evil men in the swamp trying to kill them. *Which, after all, is a fairly good summary.*

"Watchers find them, ambush them," he suggested.

"One of them will be on guard at all times, night or day," Jesse said. "And they're brutal."

"Besides," Parvel said, "I doubt all the Watchers will be as enthusiastic as you to put their lives at risk for their former prisoners."

"I ask them," Castor said, hurrying out the door. "Help the Amarians who found the treasure."

It was a good angle to use, at least, but Jesse agreed with Parvel. As much as he wished the giants would attack and subdue Captain Demetri, he had a feeling they would be doing this alone.

"We have no hope of rescuing the other two," Silas said, shaking his head. "Captain Demetri knows we're coming. You said so yourself. They will be waiting, ready to kill their two hostages if we do not surrender to them."

"Silas is right," Rae said.

Now, Jesse thought, *life is back to normal. Rae and Silas against Jesse and Parvel.*

"Either we die trying to save two, or the six of us escape alive," Silas reasoned, as if the situation were a simple mathematic equation. "We can't save everyone, Parvel."

We can't save Leisel. The thought brought a familiar ache in Jesse's stomach. There were so many names in the Forbidden Book, so many young people they could no longer save. *What if Nero and Talia are two of them?*

But Parvel was not convinced. "We have to try," he insisted. "As long as they are alive, there is still hope. And we are that hope."

"We can't do it alone," Barnaby said. "It's impossible."

"What about your family?" Parvel reminded him. "Is there not a chance they will join us?"

"His family?" Jesse asked, confused.

"He released Zora. She's trained to return to the Kin, then come back to her master," Parvel said.

Jesse and Owen exchanged glances. "I knew that stupid bird was up to something," Owen muttered.

"They will not come," Barnaby said flatly.

"You don't really believe that," Parvel said.

Jesse didn't share in his optimism. He remembered Tomas' words: "Maybe he *did* know exactly what would happen when he left. Maybe he wanted to be cut off from the Kin—from us."

"Why would you send Zora away if you had no hope that your family would come?" Parvel pressed.

"Because I didn't want her to die with us," Barnaby practically shouted in his face.

Parvel fell silent.

"Don't you understand?" Barnaby asked, fists clenched at his side. "When I joined the Guard, I left the Kin. They are not my family anymore. I am dead to them."

"We met your family," Jesse said, not sure whether now was the right time to bring that up. "Some of them wanted you to come home, and—"

"*Some* of them," Barnaby said. "So you say. But none of them came with you."

No one had anything to say to that. Jesse felt as if their last hope had been taken away from them.

He glanced over at Owen, who was being uncharacteristically silent. "What about you, Owen?" Jesse prompted.

Owen looked uncomfortable as they all stared at him. "I want to leave here," he said, "but I don't want to leave *them* here."

"Three for, three against," Rae said, sighing loudly. "Of course."

"We need to get some rest," Silas said, giving a significant look at Parvel. "All of us. We can decide then what we will do."

Rest sounded good to Jesse. Perhaps when he woke up, his head would stop pounding and everything would seem simpler. Somehow, though, he doubted it.

Barnaby was the last to leave the room. "Wait," Jesse said.

Barnaby stopped, still staying as far away from Jesse's bed as possible. "Yes?"

"I have something of yours," Jesse said, taking the token from around his neck. "Your family gave it to me."

For a moment, Barnaby just looked at it. Then he put it around his neck. "The only family I have left is Zora, if she even comes back." He started to leave again.

Jesse took a deep breath. "I just want to say that I shouldn't have shouted at you back in the prison. What I said…you didn't deserve it. I'm sorry."

"Don't be," Barnaby said, turning away. "You were right. I abandoned you, just like I abandoned them."

Somehow, Jesse knew it was as close to an apology as he would ever get from Barnaby. "I've already forgiven you for that," he said, and as soon as he said it, he knew it was true.

"They won't forgive me," Barnaby said bitterly. "The Kin never forgives—especially not Tomas. Everything to him was about following the rules, about being loyal to the Kin. Even when we were younger, he was the responsible one, the one everyone depended on. He's determined to be an elder in the Kin someday."

Jesse could picture that: Tomas making decisions and enforcing the laws.

"He'll be good at it too, I suppose," Barnaby said, shrugging. "He's good at everything."

How sad, Jesse thought. *Both Tomas and Barnaby were jealous of each other*. He started to say, "Your brother—"

"No," Barnaby said, turning away. "He's not my brother anymore."

Chapter 18

When Jesse woke up, he found Owen talking to Castor in the front room, as if nothing had happened in the past two days, although he knew the opposite was true. "More Amarian lessons?" he asked dryly.

Owen nodded. "I taught him another new word."

"What was it, 'annoying?'" Jesse asked.

"No," Castor said. "Report." He looked warily at Owen. "Report means I say what I do and see?"

"Yes," Jesse said. "For once, Owen taught you the right thing." Owen made a face at him.

"My report is Head Watcher said no to attack on evil men," Castor said. "I go out anyway, watch them all last night. See their camp, count evil men." He paused. "There are three. One is a woman."

Something about the woman had clearly disturbed Castor, because he shivered. "She sayed to other two men—"

"Said," Jesse corrected automatically.

A glare from Castor told him that it was not the time for a grammar lesson. "She said that someone was watching."

"But she didn't find you?" Jesse asked, although he was sure Castor would not be standing there if she had. Riders didn't seem to care who they killed.

"No," Castor said. "I ran away. Watchers are silent as the swamp frog."

Owen laughed at that. "I think you mean fog," Jesse corrected, stepping on Owen's foot.

"I tell Silas and others where they are, and everything about the camp and people in it," Castor continued. "It is out in swamp."

"How far out?" Jesse asked.

Castor bit his lip, clearly trying to remember words for distance. "Hour of walk? I cannot remember how to say far in lengths, except Westlund lengths."

"Very good," Jesse said. Silas and Parvel would come up with a plan. That's what they were best at. For now, Jesse was content to follow their instructions.

Castor stood, looking around the room sadly.

"You're leaving, aren't you?" Owen asked.

It wasn't a hard conclusion to make. Castor's quarters were bare. He, like the other Westlunders, had packed his things, ready for the long trip back. All that was left was one pack that came up to Jesse's neck.

Castor nodded. "Caravan leaves soon. All Watchers go back to Westlund. We will no come back."

He picked up the pack from the ground. "I carry this my own," he said, hefting it on his back with a grunt.

"Myself," Jesse corrected.

Castor nodded and pointed to the pack. "Books, paper, key and food," he explained.

"All very important things," Jesse agreed.

He was just about to ask where *his* key was, when a giant ran into the room, blurting something in agitated Westlundish. He and Castor spoke for a while, then the man hurried away. Castor turned to them. "The Lidians return," he said. "The Watchers must leave. Protect people in Westlund, for if they attack us."

"The Lidians?" Owen said, confused. "Not…ghosts?"

Castor apparently didn't know this word, because he only shrugged. "We leave now, with treasures. You go up and meet Lidians. They asked for you. For Barnaby."

Barnaby. Of course. The Westlunders would call the Kin by their old name, the Lidians. *So they did come!* Jesse felt something like hope growing in him.

"Good-bye, Owen," Castor said, patting him on the head. "Careful. Listen to Jesse."

"Not all the time," Owen said, grinning. "Then I'd never have any fun."

Then it was Jesse's turn. "Good-bye, Jesse," Castor said, nearly crushing him with a hug. "I read the book. Maybe, when I learn to write Amarian, I send a letter from Westlund!"

Jesse laughed at the thought that a letter written by a giant would manage to find its way to him, as he wandered around the kingdom as an outlaw. "Maybe," was all he said. "Good-bye, Castor. We wait for the circle moon."

"No," Castor said, shaking his head. "I am not a Watcher now. I wait for no moon. I wait for the dawn."

He waved good-bye one last time before shouldering his pack and backing into the tunnels.

Jesse hated knowing he would probably never see Castor again. He wasn't even sure he and the others would live to another dawn. *But, I suppose that's part of being a member of the Youth Guard.*

By the time Jesse and Owen went up the stairs and out of the palace, Silas, Parvel and Rae were already waiting on the porch. Down the steps, a small crowd of men stood at attention, perhaps three dozen of them, all wearing the patterned clothing of the Kin, and all armed. Jesse knew that if he were close enough to see, each of them would have a token around his neck.

Jesse studied them. None of them seemed openly hostile, but some didn't look happy to be there. He followed their eyes to see what they were looking at.

It was Barnaby, Zora on his shoulder again, surrounded by a circle of older men.

A shake of Parvel's head told him to stay away, but Jesse pretended he hadn't seen it, edging closer to the group. He had to know what was going to happen.

"There are two innocent young people being held prisoner in the swamps," Barnaby was saying. "I respectfully ask your aid in rescuing them."

"We cannot risk our lives for the sake of the king's Youth Guard," one man snapped. "It is not the Kin's way." Apparently, someone—Barnaby, or perhaps Parvel—had explained what had happened.

"We elders will discuss among ourselves," the oldest

of the men said. "You have put us in a difficult situation, young man."

"I know," Barnaby said, shame creeping into his voice, though he made no apology. Jesse tried to imagine what it would be like to face the group of people you had abandoned.

All of the men except Ravvi left and sat in a group on the steps. "Not all of the elders came," Ravvi said. "A few of them refused to have anything to do with the rescue."

"To be honest, Father, I'm surprised to see you here," Barnaby said.

Ravvi put his hand on Barnaby's shoulder. "I knew you would send Zora only in a time of greatest danger. And you are still my son."

"And Tomas?" Barnaby asked, scanning the faces in the palace courtyard.

Ravvi shook his head. "He stayed with the rest of the Kin."

For a moment, Jesse saw an expression of sadness pass over Barnaby's face, but then it hardened. "Of course." He raised his hand in a kind of salute to his father. "I will leave and let the elders decide."

Strange that he would give up so easily, Jesse thought. *After all, these are his people, and he doesn't seem the type to surrender in an argument.*

Then again, Barnaby's squad didn't seem to be as loyal to each other as Jesse's. *Maybe he doesn't really care what happens to Nero and Talia.*

"Please," Parvel said, stepping forward, "if you will let me explain the seriousness of the situation—"

But Ravvi just shook his head. "If you would speak further,

you must speak to the elders of the Kin," he said, gesturing to the group on the steps. "I do not have the power to decide."

Jesse knew from the look in Parvel's eyes that he would speak further. He loved any chance for debate, even in front of an audience. *Especially in front of an audience*, Jesse thought.

"If I may, I have something to say," Parvel said, stepping toward the elders, but speaking loud enough for the crowd to hear. "There are two young people, barely more than children, who need your help." He gestured to the gathered Kin. "Here, I see forty strong, able-bodied men. Will none of you come to their defense?"

"In our laws, you do not have permission to address the elders, young Amarian," the one elder said in a thin, reedy voice.

"Besides, you speak foolishness," a sour-faced elder added, glaring at Parvel. "We should leave at once, with or without the boy."

"Surely you can see that this is an injustice," Parvel continued, ignoring him. "Will you let innocent blood be shed in your land?"

"It is not our land anymore," an elder said, shaking his head sadly. "It fell from our hands long, long ago."

"You mean we gave it up," another voice said. Jesse turned. It was Barnaby, Zora perched on his shoulder. He was leaning against one of the pillars, looking down at the people. "Our fathers abandoned this place. They ran away when they should have fought."

"How dare you speak of our ancestors that way!" the sour-faced elder said, shaking his fist. "We never should have come to the aid of this impudent boy!" A muttering from the crowd told Jesse that many agreed with him.

"Barnaby..." Parvel said in a warning tone.

"Trust me," he said quietly. Then he turned back to the Kin. "I mean no disrespect to those who have gone before us. They did what they thought was best, but there is no need for us to repeat their mistakes."

"What do you mean, son?" Ravvi asked, stepping forward from the crowd.

"Don't you see?" Barnaby said. "The Watchers of Westlund have left Lidia behind. Here, we have a chance to reclaim what was once ours. We can rebuild. All groups of Kin, scattered around the kingdom, can join and become what they once were: Lidians. United."

The crowd began to mutter again, but this time, their hushed words were tinged with excitement. Even some of the elders appeared to be listening.

Is it really possible? Jesse wondered, looking doubtfully around at the ruins. The tunnels, at least, seemed to be past repair, soon to be destroyed by the rising waters. The rest of the city was in disrepair. He wondered if Barnaby actually thought Lidia could be rebuilt, or if he was merely using the idea as bait to manipulate the Kin.

"Amarias has rejected us. The Amarians have done nothing to welcome us, but let us wander their land, barely surviving," Barnaby said, his voice growing stronger as he paced along the porch. "We owe them no debt. Let us leave them and become a nation once again. Let us restore Lidia to her former greatness!"

A few of the Kin actually cheered at that. "The boy's right," Jesse heard one voice shout.

"That attitude was what caused the fall of Lidia in the first place," a new voice said, this one from behind them.

While all of the people watched, Tomas stepped forward, next to Barnaby, barely giving him a glance before addressing the people again. "What my brother seems to have forgotten is that this talk of rising as a great nation led the Lidians of this city to neglect its defenses, to ignore warnings of attack. It led to our downfall."

A visible conflict broke out among the people. Some sided with Tomas, while others seemed unconvinced, still excited about the prospect of rebuilding the old city.

Jesse stepped forward and spoke quietly to him. "Tomas, is this really what you want? Two could die because of your pride!"

But Tomas only brushed Jesse aside, carefully watching the crowd below.

"Is this what you young people have brought to us?" the sour-faced elder bellowed, shaking his fist at them. "Disorder and conflict to tear the Kin apart, we who have stayed together for two hundred years of exile?"

Barnaby started to speak, but Tomas cut him off. "No," he said, raising a hand to silence the people. Amazingly, the clamor of voices died down. "I agree with my brother that we must return here."

Now even Jesse wanted to join the mutterings of disbelief. *What does he mean?*

"No, I'm saying we must not focus on our glory and

pride," Tomas continued. "Doing so would distract us from danger. But this was our city, our home, and with hard work and time, we can make it so again."

"And what about these invaders, these three agents of the king who bring evil into our land?" Barnaby challenged him. "We cannot wait for hard work and time to get rid of them. We must act now."

"With caution, following the tradition of the Kin, we will drive them from here," Tomas said, speaking more to the crowd than his brother. "According to our laws, we can go to war against anyone who threatens even one of our own."

"He is not our own anymore," a dissenter shouted. "When he joined the Guard, he left the Kin."

There was silence in the crowd. Not even Ravvi protested.

Jesse remembered all that Tomas and Barnaby had said. *"Maybe he wanted to be cut off from the Kin." "The Kin never forgives." "I am dead to them."*

Then the oldest elder stood shakily. "No," he said. He climbed the stairs with effort and stood between Barnaby and Tomas. "We have a law—rarely used, but present from the earliest days of our people. A son of Lidia can always return."

There was no sound of any kind from the crowd. Everyone was watching, waiting. The elder turned to Barnaby. "The only question is: do you choose to return?"

For a moment, Barnaby hesitated. Then he stepped forward. "My brother is right. Pride can only destroy. It was because of pride that I left the Kin. But now I return, and so can this fallen city!"

More cheers this time, and Jesse noted there were very few skeptics left in the group.

"Zeal, order and wisdom on the same platform," one of the other elders mused, once the noise had died down. "Never since the day of Jardos, Vincent, and Hyram."

It was true, Jesse realized. The three men addressing the people looked very little like the three men of the statues, yet they fulfilled their roles: Barnaby to inspire, Tomas to plan carefully, and the elder to offer counsel. *Lidia has found its leaders again.*

"I, Tomas, son of Lidia, call a ruling session of elders in keeping with the laws of the Kin," Tomas said. Immediately, all of the people began to sit down.

Out of respect, Jesse guessed. *He must be invoking some official procedure.* Parvel made a motion for his fellow squad members to sit, and Jesse did so, even though the marble of the porch was still wet with rain.

"I make a motion that we go to war against these three Riders, for the safety of our people," Tomas said. As soon as he finished speaking, he too sat.

"I am the fourth generation from Nolan, son of Hyram," the elder between Tomas and Barnaby said, his old bones creaking as he stood. "I second the motion. All elders in attendance who support this, stand."

At first, no one moved. Then one elder stood, reaching to help the man beside him to his feet. Another elder, looking up at them, got a determined look on his face and stood. Soon, all but one of the elders were standing.

"It is enough," Tomas said, triumph in his voice. "The motion is passed."

"Tonight, we fight, as our ancestors would not," Barnaby called. "Tonight, we fight for Lidia!" A cheer rose from the gathered Kin, and the men drew their swords, holding them up in salute.

"We wait for nightfall," Parvel called, once the noise had died down. "Come back here when the sun sets."

The assembled men were quick to disperse, leaving the courtyard in different directions. Jesse knew the excitement of exploring the ruins, but he couldn't imagine how excited he would be if he knew his people would be rebuilding them soon.

Only Tomas and Barnaby did not move to join their countrymen.

"Well, I see you haven't lost your gift for moving a crowd," Tomas said dryly, arms folded as he faced his brother.

"And you're just as set on order and regulations," Barnaby countered. "What are you doing here, Tomas? Father said—"

"I left after the others," Tomas said, cutting him off. "I felt it was my duty to join them." A small smile appeared on his face. "Besides, I missed the bird."

"Well, you can have her," Owen piped up. "I certainly don't want her around." In response, Zora screeched at him.

"Well, what are we going to do for the next few hours?" Jesse asked Owen. "I've had quite enough of exploring this city. I practically know it better than my own hometown."

Owen started jumping down the steps two at a time. "Let's

go to the treasure tree," he said. "We can try to find something the giants missed."

Jesse just shook his head. He should have known Owen would suggest something like that. "We'll be back," he called to Parvel, Silas and Rae. Parvel smiled and waved him on.

"Maybe we'll find the other two silver keys," Jesse said, following Owen down the steps at a much slower pace.

"Didn't you check your pocket?" Owen asked.

"No," Jesse said, but his hand immediately went to it. He pulled out his silver key, wrapped in a piece of paper.

"Castor got them out," Owen said. "In a room full of treasure, burning to the ground, he took time to take three keys out of a lock."

Jesse unfolded the paper. It was a picture of a compass. The printing at the bottom read, "C is for Compass." Jesse grinned. *I bet there's now a page missing from Castor's primary reader.*

Above the drawing, written in Castor's neat writing, was a single word: "Promise." Jesse turned it over. On the back, Castor had written, "You are not a son of Lidia, but you are a brother."

Jesse held it out to Owen. "Did you see this?"

He nodded. "I helped him with spelling. We had a lesson on the alphabet. The Westlundish version is a little different than ours."

Jesse took another look at the compass in the drawing. "Look," he said, his voice rising in excitement, pointing to its center.

"It's a needle," Owen said without enthusiasm. "Most compasses have them."

"No, it's Parvel's golden dial, the one that pointed us to the palace," Jesse said. "I recognize it. The Lidians must have had a large compass made of gold, and the broken dial was the needle that pointed north."

"And the compass probably burnt down with the rest of the treasures," Owen said, pointing. "Right there."

They had reached the tree, or what was left of the tree. It had fallen into one of the nearby buildings, crushing its roof. *Another rebuilding project for the Kin*, Jesse thought.

Owen scrambled up the fallen trunk, not seeming to care that he was getting ash all over his shirt. "Come on, Jesse," he called.

Jesse shook his head. "I've had enough climbing, thank you."

He missed Castor being there to add, "You're welcome."

Owen emerged a few minutes later, empty handed. "Not even a coin," he said dismally. "Those giants did a good job."

"Maybe when the Kin move the tree, they'll find something," Jesse said.

"But I won't be here then," Owen pointed out.

"Maybe you will be," Jesse said. He had been giving it a lot of thought. Now he just had to explain to Owen. "You could stay here, you know—you, Nero and Talia. It would be safer than anywhere else in Amarias. Once you join the Youth Guard, you're a marked man for the rest of your life."

"But I don't think the Kin, or the Lidians, or whatever I'm

supposed to call them really want us here," Owen said. "They don't seem to like outsiders."

Jesse shrugged. "Some do, some don't, just like any other group of people. But Barnaby could convince them, I'm sure. It would be a nice place to live."

Owen just shrugged. "But what about my family?" Suddenly, he looked small again, and Jesse wondered what would make an eleven-year-old boy leave home to join the Youth Guard.

Jesse sighed. "That's the question all of us asked when we found out the truth." With the king trying to kill them, no place was safe, not even home—not when they could be bringing danger to others. Youth Guard members, the ones who survived, were destined to be wanderers like the Kin.

But now the Kin have found a place to call home, Jesse thought. *Maybe we can someday too.*

"And you're not going to stay here, are you?" Owen asked.

"I don't think so," Jesse said. He had seen Silas looking through the Forbidden Book, probably deciding where they would go next. As long as there were Guard members still alive, still in need of help, they would be on the move.

"Can I come with you?" Owen asked.

"No," Jesse said. For some reason, he was sure that was the right answer. He and his squad had faced death several times in the past month, and they would again. Once, he had been confident they could survive anything. Now, he realized that overconfidence was just another form of pride. They were playing a dangerous game, defying the Riders. He wanted to protect Owen from that.

"Will you ever come back?" Owen pressed.

How could Jesse answer that? The paper in his hand reminded him that promises, even ones made to give hope to an eleven-year-old, were not to be made lightly.

"I don't know," he finally said. "I don't know where I'll be tomorrow, or what will happen to me. But if I can, I'll find a way to get you back home to your family, even if I have to fight the entire kingdom to do it."

He didn't know where the words came from. From God, maybe, because all Jesse had been concerned about for the past month was living another day. He hadn't the time to think about what might happen next, what they would do after they had exhausted the list of names in the Forbidden Book.

Could we really ignore all the injustice we've seen and go back to a normal life? Jesse knew the answer was no. He and his squad would not quietly disappear into the pages of history, like the Lidians, never to be heard of again. They would not be among the Vanished. For as long as they could, they would fight.

Owen was still looking up at him, waiting. "And I'll never forget you," Jesse added. "I promise."

"Because we're brothers, right?" Owen asked, scrambling down from the tree to stand beside him. "Castor said so."

Jesse nodded. "Yes. Because we're brothers."

CHAPTER 20

The nightmares had come back.

Demetri was running, running toward the camp. *Too late, too late, too late*, his pulse shouted with every step. He could see the soldiers moving in the dark. They would kill Desma, Uric and Benjamin in their sleep. And it was his fault.

He stumbled down the hill into the tents. There were shouts, torches, the smell of smoke, chaos and noise and the clang of metal against metal. Everything was a blur.

"Stop!" his hoarse voice shouted. "I didn't mean to do it! Stop!" He stumbled forward blindly, panic numbing him. "For God's sake, stop!"

But God, if He were listening, did nothing to stop the attack.

"Run!" someone shouted. A woman's voice. Desma?

Again, "Run, Demetri!"

Demetri? Desma would have called him Justis. Even in his dreamy haze, Demetri was sure of that. Then, slowly, he realized he was no longer asleep. A boot kicked his side. "Get up! We're being attacked."

Lillen's voice—Demetri recognized it now. He jerked upright, threw off his blanket. The noises of attack were real and close. *But how had the Four mustered an army?*

There was no time to wonder—only to run. Lillen was gone. He took his sword, nothing else. The crossbow would be no good in the close quarters of a surprise attack.

Once he was outside the tent, Ward ran past him. "Do not fight," he ordered. "Run."

Demetri was not used to running. It was cowardly.

But one look at the force descending on the camp changed his mind. There were dozens of them, at least, rushing toward them with torches and swords. Somewhere, a horn sounded, calling the army of the Four into battle.

He ran.

It was still dark, and therefore hard for Demetri to find solid footing. Lillen, however, didn't seem concerned about falling into a pit. She ran hard and strong, and Demetri and Ward tried to follow in her footsteps.

The noise behind them told Demetri they were being followed. He tightened his grip on his sword and scanned the area for a good defensive position. There was none.

"They have the two Youth Guard hostages," Lillen called back, between gasps of breaths. "They will not follow us far."

Lillen was right. Once they had gone a distance into the swamps, their pursuers pulled back, letting them go. *A wise choice.* It would be foolish to chase them into the swamps. Three might avoid the tar pits and quicksand; an entire army would not.

Still, they kept running until Demetri was sure his side would split open. "Far enough," Lillen said, leaning against a tree. "They will not come here."

"Three Riders running from their victims," Ward said, sounding disgusted. Of all of them, he seemed the least tired, barely breathing heavily. He clutched his arm, and Demetri noticed for the first time a red stain seeping through his shirt.

For such a slight man, Demetri realized, *he is strong in his own way*.

Demetri asked the question that had been on his mind all the time they ran. "Who was on watch? Who guarded the hostages at the time of the attack?" He knew there was an accusation in his tone, and he didn't bother to hide it.

"I was coming to relieve Lillen," Ward said. "They picked the perfect moment, when our guard was down. Somehow, they knew our schedule exactly." Ward shook his head. "I don't understand it."

He ripped off a piece of cloth from the bottom of his cloak and began to tie it around his wound.

"I tell you, there was someone watching us last night," Lillen insisted, steel in her voice. "A spy. We should have killed the hostages then as I suggested, instead of waiting to be attacked."

Demetri had been the one to block her order to kill the two hostages. It was too soon, he'd said. They could fight off the Four when they came to rescue the hostages.

He had been wrong…again.

"But you didn't fight?" Demetri demanded. Lillen, at least, seemed eager to shed blood.

"I fight to win," Lillen said. "We could not win, not against so many."

It was true, Demetri knew, but, all the same, he was not eager to hear the verdict. "I would have taken at least one."

"You were dead asleep in your tent when they attacked," Ward shot back. "If not for us, you would have been slaughtered."

"Peace," Lillen said. "No one is to blame. The Four are even stronger than we thought. They have awakened the Kin of Lidia, who have long been passive wanderers. It is not good for us—for Amarias—that they have been united again."

"The Four will leave the swamps," Ward said. "We will as well." He began to walk, and though Demetri had lost his own sense of direction days before, he followed him.

"And where will they go?" Demetri demanded of Lillen this time. When it came to things that had not yet happened, the priestess was the one to ask.

She hesitated. Demetri did not like that hesitation. Lillen was always confident, often too confident. "One of two places."

"And those places are?"

"The ports of District One, outside the capital," she said, "or the battlegrounds of the War of the Northern Waste. Those are the last-known locations of the only surviving Youth Guard squads."

Demetri groaned, a map of the kingdom appearing in his mind, every detail in place just as he had memorized it. "Those are on opposite sides of the kingdom!"

"I will ask for a vision of where they are going," Lillen said. "We travel quickly. We will get there before them."

"And what if there is no vision?" Demetri challenged. "Tell me, Lillen, did you see a vision of our attack tonight? Did you foresee losing our two hostages and fleeing from the Four we were sent to destroy?"

"I can only see what the Great One wishes me to see," Lillen snapped. Her eyes seemed to stab at him like daggers, and Demetri felt the medallion grow cold against his chest, a cold that somehow burned him. He remembered suddenly why he had been afraid of the slender, pale woman.

"In a way he is right, Lillen," Ward said smoothly. "For whatever reason, the Great One seems to have left this mission largely to us, without his supernatural insights. As you have said before, they are protected."

"Yes," Lillen said, though it came out more as a hiss. "The Enemy is strong in them, and getting stronger every day. Soon, they will all be His."

"Not if we destroy them first," Ward said, and his tone seemed to soothe her somehow.

"But we don't know where we're going," Demetri reminded them. "What if we pick one location and are wrong? It would take weeks to find them again, if we ever did."

"We only have to be in one place, right or wrong," Ward said, a smug smile appearing on his face. "We travel to District One. There we can report to the Rider Council and wait for the Four."

"And if they go instead to the Northern Waste?" Demetri challenged.

"Never fear, Captain," Ward said lightly. "If they go to rescue the squad on the front, I know exactly where they will be and to whom they will go. The Riders have many contacts, including several on the battlefields. I will send a message at once. If they arrive at the Northern Waste, they will not be among friends."

"Yes," Lillen said, nodding. "I know of whom you speak. One man in particular will know how to bring down the Four."

"The way we've been trying to bring them down?" Demetri asked. "We have not gotten good results, if you recall, Lillen."

She turned her merciless eyes on him again, and he couldn't meet them. "If these are the Four of the prophecy, they will not be destroyed with mighty force or cunning traps," Lillen said. "Long have I known this."

That was too much for Demetri. "Then why are we here? If you're right, there is nothing more we can do."

Lillen didn't appear to be disturbed in the least by his outburst. "But there is," she said. "They can bring *each other* down. I, or the Rider of whom Ward speaks, can force them to do this."

"Yes," Ward said, nodding thoughtfully. "It will be more difficult, of course, but far more rewarding. No matter which way they go, they go to their deaths—by the hands of their own squad members."

The plan didn't seem plausible to Demetri. He had seen nothing but the deepest loyalty from the Four. They seemed willing to give their lives for each other. Their actions were foolish, of course, but he could remember a time when he would have done the same for the few he loved. He doubted Lillen and Ward had such a memory. *And so they underestimate the loyalty of the Four.*

He opened his mouth to say so, then stopped. *They would not listen to me anyway. If we fail, so be it. We fail by their hands, not mine.*

"How will we do it?" was all he asked.

"We promise each one of them what they want most," Lillen said. The smile on her face might have been deeply peaceful, if not for the glint of evil in her eyes. "The price? A betrayal of the other three."

"Most often, what a person wants most is something that can't be given to him," Demetri said, feeling a familiar pang deep inside. He briefly saw his mother, then young Parvel, then Desma. Her face lingered longer than the others, and Demetri was sure she was looking straight at him from beyond the grave.

Then her face turned into Lillen's, looking at him with those searching blue eyes. "Perhaps not. But it can be promised to them."

"A lie, then."

"I am a daughter of lies," Lillen said, shrugging. "Promises mean nothing to me."

"And what would you promise them?" Ward asked. "What could possibly be important enough that they would betray their friends?"

In answer, Lillen began to sing, starting quietly and rising in volume, the eerie notes seeming to hang in the night air before fading away. "Not all who vanish are truly lost. Not all that is missing is gone. Some melt away like the morning frost. Some will return come the dawn."

Demetri let out a breath and was surprised to realize he hadn't been breathing. There was something about those words.... They seemed to promise him everything he had ever wanted but missed, everyone he had ever loved and lost.

"It is an old, old song," Lillen said, "sung in different forms by our own since the dawn of time. There are other verses, unknown to the Lidians. We taught them the one that would appeal to them, and I believe it will appeal to our Four as well."

She continued humming the tune, and Demetri felt everything in him leaning in closer to hear every ancient, beautiful note.

When he looked up again, he was staring at the dead moss of the swamp, alone. He saw movement ahead and hurried to catch up with Lillen and Ward. *Do I really want to travel with them?*

He reached inside his shirt and took his Rider medallion off. Even though it was fairly light, Demetri felt like a pressing weight had been taken from his chest. He stared at the surface: the symbol of Amarias inside the broken circle, and around the border, the dragon. The Great One. A wave of doubt swept over him. *What have I done? Who have I become?*

Demetri knew he was not as upset as he should be that the Four had escaped. In a way, he was beginning to respect them, but he would not pity them. He had sworn to destroy them, and he would fulfill his vow.

Looking back into the swamp one last time, he thought,

it will be interesting to see what they do next. He was beginning to realize that he did not want to kill the Four. Perhaps he never had.

The realization startled him so much he put the medallion back on, quickly. Aleric had hinted that the medallion had some kind of power—that much Demetri knew. At times it seemed to cloud his mind, at other times it gave him great strength. Now Demetri wondered if it could sense betrayal.

He shivered and told himself it was because of the wet cold, but he couldn't deny that here in the swamps, he felt more dead than alive. Even the medallion around his neck couldn't distract him from the dull longing that still beat hollowly in his chest.

No, he was not sure if God—who Lillen, Doran and Aleric called "the Enemy"—existed. But, for the first time, he was sure the Great One was real, that there was a power of darkness he had aligned himself with.

If Lillen was to be trusted—in spiritual matters, and Demetri believed she was—this power, this darkness, was angry with him. With his failure. That was why the medallion no longer gave him strength. He was sure of it. Now, every movement was like a struggle against an oppressive fog, thicker than the mist of the swamp. He was already one of the Vanished.

Not all who vanish are truly lost.

The thought came without warning, only this time not in Lillen's soft, chilling alto. Instead, it sounded like a simple straightforward message, like something true—a light through the darkness of the swamp.

He pushed the thought away. He had chosen to be lost when he joined the Riders. Something had been stolen from him then: his soul, perhaps, if he were willing to believe such a thing existed.

And, if his soul was lost, he despaired of ever getting it back.